The Orphan's Lost Soul

Sophia Watts

Contents

Chapter One

Peter Chalmers took great pride in his work at the gentleman's club.

While there were many who did not prefer to work in such an exclusive club, finding the task of being forced to interact with the upper class and held to a higher standard to be too taxing. Peter, on the other hand, did not agree with that sentiment.

Why, he flourished in such an environment given his own military history. He had spent a few years in the military and had been well on his way to rising through the ranks were it not for the Indian mutiny that left him with a leg injury. Most days, he scarcely noticed the limp, having grown used to it, but now and again, he felt people glance his way, pity shining in their eyes.

It only made him stand up straighter and hold his head high.

Considering the fact that he was injured while fighting for his country, Peter knew he had nothing to be ashamed of. Not when he had fought with honour and dignity and been rewarded with a respectable job in lieu of being left to fend for himself on the street. Given that his childhood sweetheart had been anxiously awaiting his return, Peter had taken the offer without a second thought. It brought him a great deal of comfort and joy, particularly as the environment was all too familiar to him.

Members of the gentleman's club were senior officers who came from well-to-do families and needed the social retreat to unwind. Although Peter himself was not allowed the use of the facilities, he had often studied the club and the services it offered, from the well-stocked library room to the restaurants that catered to the whim of its clients. There were even rooms in order for the gentleman in question to engage in a game of cards or billiards.

And the entire establishment often reeked of drink and covered in thick plumes of smoke that clung to Peter's clothes long after he returned home to his wife. Rosie, his beloved wife of twenty-and-some years, rarely complained, if ever, but he saw the wrinkle of her nose when he walked in, and felt her hesitation when he leaned in to hug her.

In truth, his wife deserved a far better life than the one he was providing for her. On many days, when she had long since gone to bed, he stood watching her bathed her in the soft halo of the moon and felt a familiar ache in the centre of his chest. As a young and ambitious lad on the brink of greatness, Peter had allowed himself to dream of a great many things.

Including a fine life for himself and Rosie.

The two of them had grown up right next to each other, with their mothers spending long hours together, tending to their duties and leaving them to play together. By the time he was ten-years-old, Rosie had become a dear friend to him, and he spent hours in her presence. At fourteen years of age, he had known there was no other woman for him and had all but declared himself to her, only waiting for employment in order to be able to formally make her his wife.

His prayers had been answered in the form of the military draft.

Rosie had been tearful when he had told her of his plans to go off and fight. He recalled that particular day with perfect clarity, and the tears that fell on her rosy cheeks. Peter had ached to hold her against him, to stroke her chestnut-coloured hair away from her face and offer her the comfort she needed. Unfortunately, propriety had done little but allow him to stand across from her with his hands clasped behind his back. Tearfully, she had bidden him farewell some days later, standing in the doorway to their room, with her mother standing behind her, a hand on her shoulders.

Peter had never forgotten the solemn look on her face.

It had stayed with him throughout the war.

For years, the memory had chased him, never leaving him a moment's rest. In the dead of night, while the other soldiers slept around him, he would crawl out of the tent and bring his body to rest against the ground underneath a blanket of stars. A few of the other men had shaken their heads and snickered at him, wondering why he chose to leave himself exposed to a brusque wind and the comfortable ground.

Even now, Peter struggled to explain it to them.

All he had known was that being out in the open, with nothing but foliage for miles on end, filled him with a sense of comfort. And tilting his head back to take in the night sky made him feel closer to Rosie. He'd imagined her looking up at the same sky and thinking of him, the distance between them growing smaller and smaller. On the days when his muscles screamed in protest and his heart ached for her, Peter touched a hand to his chest and felt the locket hanging there with Rosie's picture concealed within.

It had gotten him through long days and cold nights.

When the others had convinced him to sleep in the tent, rather than freeze outside in the cold, he would take the locket out and hold it gently in the palm of his hands. Over and over, he had stroked her picture and murmured her name underneath his breath. Rosie had been a great beauty, with hair the colour of chestnuts and eyes the colour of warm honey. He'd often feared returning home to find her married to another, but it was his steadfast devotion to her, and the love they had for each other, that kept him going.

Until he returned to her, some years later, heavy with exhaustion and grief. Rosie had been speechless for a few moments before she had ushered him inside. Her mother had welcomed him back with a gentle smile and a cup of warm tea. For hours, Peter had remained huddled in an old wooden chair in front of the fireplace, studying the flames that leapt and danced before his eyes.

With a slight shake of his head, Peter chased the memory away and straightened his back. The streets were quiet and largely empty save for the occasional men who stumbled out of bars, deep in their cups, red faced, and bellowing loudly. As soon as they approached him, he took a step to the side and allowed them to pass. A few of them smiled at him, their gazes glazed and empty. He resumed his walk and tightened his jacket around his waist.

The evening breeze was not cold, but there was a nip in the air, and he was eager to get back home to Rosie, a warm fireplace, and the delicious meal waiting for him. Each step took him closer and closer to his home, while the city around him slept largely undisturbed by the comings and goings of the outside world.

Truthfully, it was his favourite time of night.

There was little to be expected from him at present.

Back at the gentleman's club, there were others to tend to the officers and serve at their beck and call. Come morning, he was expected to return and perform his duties, but for now, he was a free man able to tend to his own needs and those of his wife. At times, Peter wondered if he could change his own fate and strike out on his own. After he had been forced to take his leave of the military, he had imagined himself as a blacksmith. For a short time, he had imagined himself owning his own shop and hiring young men to be his apprentices.

Alas, his injury had prevented him from pursuing that dream.

Instead, Peter had been forced to turn to the gentlemen's club in search of a way to survive. He made a decent living, and they treated him well, but Peter was acutely aware of the difference between himself and the officers he served. Although they were well respected establishments, and many thought of it as an honour to work there, there was no denying that employees were held to the highest standards of conduct. None of them were allowed to answer back to the clients, save to recommend spirits or other refreshments. Other than that, they were expected to be silent and keep to themselves little more than spectres in the hallowed halls.

Still, it was better than the alternative.

With a wife to care for, Peter did not have the luxury of being selective when it came to his employment. Working at the gentleman's club provided him with decent, yet meagre wages, but it kept a roof over their heads, and it gave them a warm fire and food every day. As far as accommodations went, there was little else he could ask for. Lately, he had taken it upon himself to find other means of employment, in order to allow Rosie a repose, but it had not been easy.

His wife was employed as a seamstress, working from their modest dwellings. While she was hard working and dedicated, he saw the toll it took on her. Like her mother before her, Rosie had taken to it from a young age and continued well into adulthood. She did not possess the same speed and dexterity she did when she had been a younger woman, but Rosie still applied herself with a great deal of vigour and concentration. Day in and day out, he saw her bent over the clothes, working until her fingers bled, and her eyes were strained.

Many times, he returned home only to find her breakfast untouched on a plate next to her. Still, she made the time to tend to her other duties, including dinner, and for that, he was immensely grateful. So, he often returned to pull Rosie up to her feet and offer her a much-needed respite from the tedious work of a seamstress.

Though they were far more fortunate than many, Peter could not help but dwell on their misfortunes, too.

For the most part, he was thankful, and every night when he knelt in front of the bed and clasped his hands together, he focused on all of the blessings he had been given. Starting with his health and ending with being blessed with Rosie for a wife. Yet, now and again, he could not help but wonder. With a start, Peter rounded the corner and came to a complete halt in the middle of the street.

There, on the other side of the street in the mouth of the alley, dressed in tatters and unmoving, was a woman, whose back was pressed against the wall. He could scarcely make out her features and were it not for the dress and bundle tossed onto the ground next to her, he would not have known it was a woman at all. Peter straightened his back, glanced down both sides of the street, and hurried over. When he was close enough to make out her gaunt features, he crouched in front of her and spoke in a low voice.

"Miss?"

Silence stretched.

Slowly, he reached out and touched her shoulders, only to yank his hand back moments later. She was cold to the touch, and her body collapsed onto the floor in a heap. Peter jumped backwards in surprise, and his hand flew to his chest. Above the pounding of his heart, he heard a whimper and the sound of a sniff. So, he inched away from the woman's dead body and knelt in front of the heap. After pulling aside the rags, a pair of green eyes peered up at him, and a startled gasp fell from his lips.

Peter cleared his throat. "Hello there."

The little girl crawled out from underneath the rags and stared up at him. She was covered in dirt, and the clothes that hung off her body were covered in holes. When she blinked, she wrapped her arms around herself and swayed. Then she crumpled onto the floor. At the last second, Peter reached for her and kept her from hitting the ground. He held her against him and glanced around.

But the streets were empty.

Carefully, he set her back on the street, with her back propped against the wall, and crouched in front of her. "Can you tell me your name, my dear?"

Her eyes fluttered open, and she stared at him.

"Is this your mother?" He tilted his head in the direction of the body, half inclined to shield her from it, but knowing he needed answers. After another moment, the girl gave him a small nod and shivered. Peter stood up and peeled off his jacket. When he draped it over her shoulders, she looked so small and frail, practically drowning in his jacket that his heart broke for her.

She could not have been more than four years of age.

Unfortunately, it was difficult to tell for certain, given her form and the lasting hunger in her eyes. The creature in front of him was little more than skin and bones, and after he surveyed the body lying a few feet away, he came to the conclusion that her mother had been dead for a day.

Possibly two.

For the life of him, he could not understand why no one had noticed. Given that they were in a crowded part of the city, it was inconceivable that no one had come across her on their way past. Although he did not normally take this route, she had been hard to miss, especially propped up against the wall of a dark alley, her silhouette offering a stark contrast to her empty and desolate surroundings. Bile rose in the back of his throat at the cruelty of such a dismissal, and he came to stand in front of the body, wishing to shield the little girl from its horror.

In his heart, he already knew it was too late.

The little girl had been by her mother's side while she took her last few breaths, and she had stayed, unaware of the gravity of what had befallen her. A few moments passed while Peter pondered the situation, turning it over and over in his head. Finally, having made up his mind about the matter, he held his hand out to the girl and waited. As soon as she tucked her cold hand into his, he breathed a sigh of relief and scooped her up.

Her head came to a rest against his chest, above the thudding of his heart. Peter walked quickly, eager to return home to Rosie. Once he reached the ramshackle building, he took the stairs two at a time and only stopped to catch his breath. When he burst through the door, Rosie jumped to her feet and spun around to face him. She took one look at the form in his arms and hurried over.

Rosie wiped her hands on her aprons and took the child from him. "What happened? The poor dear looks starved to death."

"I found her on the street next to her mother," Peter whispered, with a shake of his head. "It looks as if she has been dead for some time."

Rosie cursed to herself and held the girl closer to her bosom. "Lord have mercy. Why did no one stop to rescue the girl?"

Peter shrugged. "I cannot say for certain. I will go down to the constabulary right away."

Rosie nodded. "I will bathe and feed the poor child."

Peter touched his wife's shoulders and smiled. "You are a good woman, Rosie Chalmers."

Rosie waved his comment away. "Nonsense. It is the right thing to do, after all." She bent her head to look at the girl peering up at her with fear and uncertainty. "Don't you worry, my dear. We will take good care of you, we will. There's a good girl. Let's get you cleaned up and get some food in you."

Slowly, Rosie set the girl down on her feet. She hid behind the folds of Rosie's apron, and her small hands darted out for Rosie's. Rosie stood up straighter, and coaxed the girl away, a strange sort of gleam in her eyes. Peter stared after them for a while before leaving. On his way down the stairs, he walked slower, unable to escape the image of the wretched woman on the street.

Although he had not gotten a closer look at her, she looked to be a young woman, no more than fifteen years of age. She had clearly had nothing to her name save for the clothes on her back, and those she had used to wrap her child up in. Peter wondered if the little girl was going to have any memory of this awful night.

He prayed she would not.

What an awful memory to be saddled with.

By the time he made it to the constabulary, Peter had made up his mind to pay for the burial himself. Given the way in which she had been found, it was the least he could do as a good and devout Christian. Doubtless, no one else would come forward and offer to undertake such an expense. After a quick word with the constable, Peter led him back to the body and took a few steps back once they came to a stop in front of the alley. The constable had bent down and muttered under his breath. Then he gestured to another constable, who carried her.

Suddenly, Peter found himself following them until they reached the church. The wind around him grew brusque as they formed a circle in the graveyard, with the priest presiding over the entire affair. The woman was lowered into the ground by two men the priest had beckoned. After a quick prayer, Peter fished into his pockets and pulled out a coin.

He pitied the woman who had been laid to rest in the ground, but he took comfort in the fact that she had been given a proper burial. Still, for some unbeknownst reason, he continued to stand there studying the dirt beneath his feet. Shortly after, he made his way back home, each step feeling heavier than the last. As soon as he walked in through the door, his eyes fell to the sleeping form on the chair by the fireplace with a quilt wrapped around her shoulders.

Rosie crept towards him. "Is it done?"

Peter ran a hand through his hair. "It is done. No one knows who the poor soul was, but at least she was given a proper burial."

Rosie came to stand beside Peter and lowered her head. "May God have mercy on her soul. May her suffering finally come to an end."

Peter swallowed. "Amen."

He wrapped his arm around Rosie's shoulders and pulled her against him. She brought her head to a rest against his shoulders, and the two of them watched the even rise and fall of the sleeping girl's chest. Now that she had been cleaned and fed, the lines on her face were pronounced, as were her frail form and the gaunt look in her eyes.

Poor thing had been close to perishing, as well.

Peter shuddered at the unwelcomed thought.

What would have become of her had he not taken notice of her mother?

The knots in his stomach tightened when he realized that two bodies could've been laid to rest rather than one. He sent up a quick prayer, and Rosie stirred beside him. On the tips of their toes, they crept forward and crouched in front of the little girl. Rosie lifted a hand up and brushed her golden locks out of her face.

"I do not think she has ever been warm in her life," Rosie whispered, her breath catching towards the end. "What an awful thing that must be."

Peter reached for Rosie's hand and held it. "It is."

"And she was falling asleep while I was feeding her," Rosie continued in a quieter voice. "What will become of her, Peter?"

Peter studied the girl's face. "I expect they will send her to an orphanage."

Rosie sucked in a harsh breath. "She will not survive there. You know that as well as I."

Peter twisted to face her and saw the plea written in his wife's eyes. "What would you have me do?"

"She can stay here with us," Rosie murmured, a myriad of emotions dancing across her face. "I see no reason why she cannot. We have room, and I will take good care of her."

Peter frowned. "Will the neighbours not be suspicious?"

"We will tell them she is my sister's daughter," Rosie told him. "No one will care as long as she is not a bother. And I will ensure that she is not."

Peter squeezed Rosie's hand. "What if someone comes looking for her?"

Rosie's eyes filled with tears. "Would they not have found her by now rather than leaving her to starve and suffer on the streets?"

Peter glanced away, his chest tightening. "You are right."

Condemning her to a life in the orphanage was a far worse fate than being out on the streets. Although she would be provided with food, clothing, and shelter in the orphanage, she was also to subject to the whims of the sisters there. Truthfully, he'd heard too many stories and come across too many children who'd run away from there, finding the harsh streets of the city to be a better option than the prison walls and treatment of the orphanage.

God have mercy.

While he knew what the lawful thing to do was, Peter could not bring himself to do that to the little girl. Not after everything she had been through. By looking at her, he could tell she had suffered a great deal, as had her poor mother, and the last thing he wanted was to add to her suffering.

For the life of him, he could not.

Fortunately, the constable had not inquired after the bundle of clothes next to the woman. Nor had he seemed particularly interested in anything other than laying her to rest and returning to his duties. Peter was obliged, nay, duty bound to come clean regarding the girl he had found, but he could not.

Particularly not with Rosie pleading with him.

Over the past two decades, the two of them had tried time and again for her to be with child, but all of their efforts had failed. Now that Rosie was well past her prime, she could no longer conceive, and the doctor had advised against it, making it plain to them that she would not survive if she were to attempt it. Although it had broken their hearts to come to grips with the reality, Rosie had found ways to fill the hole inside of her. Between caring for and tending to her duties as a seamstress and wife, she did not give herself enough time to dwell.

But the Lord had seen fit to bless them after all of their hardship.

And they deserved a child of their own.

"We can keep her," Peter decided after a lengthy pause. He pulled Rosie up to her feet and took both of her hands in his. "We shall tell the neighbours that your sister passed, and we wish to take the child in as our own."

Rosie gave him a weak smile. "Can we truly keep her?"

Peter pulled her against him and stroked her hair. "I see no reason why we cannot. We can raise her as our own, and she will have a good life."

"The Lord has blessed us," Rosie murmured before bringing her head to a rest against my chest. "I can think of nothing else I would rather do."

"You will make a wonderful mother, my dear," Peter told her, before placing a kiss on top of her head. "And I feel certain that the girl will be a great source of joy and comfort to us."

Rosie stirred and drew away from him. "I feel certain that she will. Oh, my love, how fortunate we are to have found her. And for the Lord to have brought here, to our doorstep."

Together, they knelt before her and bowed their heads. When the little girl stirred, Rosie held out her arms, and she left the chair to climb into her arms. Rosie clutched the girl to her chest, and Peter saw the relief and ache written in her eyes before he glanced away. Slowly, they rose to their feet and took her into the small room in the back. Pressed against the wall was a single cot with a mattress on top. Next to it was a cot Rosie had found abandoned on the streets and brought inside in the hopes of making use of it.

He glanced towards it, then back at Rosie's face. With an infinite amount of tenderness and care, she set the little girl down and tucked her in. Her small hands darted out and gripped Rosie's as if her life depended on it. Rosie's lips lifted into a smile as she bent down and stroked the girl's face.

"Hush now, it will be alright. You can live with us, if you'd like."

The girl nodded, her bright eyes shining with unshed tears.

"I will take good care of you, my precious," Rosie told her in a hushed voice. She lowered herself onto the floor, so the two of them were at eye level. Rosie held her gaze and did not flinch or look away. "And I think the two of us shall get along very well."

The girl inched closer and squeezed her eyes shut.

A single tear slid down her cheeks.

Rosie touched her face and released a deep breath. "I know you have suffered much, but there is no need to suffer anymore. We will take good care of you, and you will be our daughter."

Peter came to stand behind Rosie and placed a hand on her shoulders. "We shall need to come up with a name for her."

Rosie covered his hand with hers, the other still gripping the girl's. "I think we should call her Lilly."

Peter smiled. "Lilly Chalmers is a beautiful name, and it suits her."

The three of them were going to be quite happy together.

He would make certain of it.

Chapter Two

Five years later…

"Mama, are you alright?"

Rosie glanced down into her daughter's bright and inquisitive face, and a smile hovered on the edges of her lips. "Yes, my pet."

Lilly frowned, her green eyes full of worry. "You must rest, Mama. You look awfully tired."

And she was, but Rosie knew she could not rest.

Not yet.

Not when there were still a great many clothes to be mended. Over the past few years, she had been teaching Lilly the tricks of the trade in order to prepare her for the real world. Someday, Lilly was going to grow up, and Rosie wanted to be sure she could provide for herself, regardless of her marital status. Like any mother, she hoped Lilly would do well enough, and she often prayed that she would be given a much better life than the one they had provided her with.

To be sure, the Chalmers had done everything they could for their darling daughter, from providing her with enough food and clothes, to insisting that she attended school with the other kids. Although Rosie had been reluctant at first, scarcely seeing the need for an education when she was unlikely to make use of it, Peter had insisted.

He did, after all, wish for his daughter to have a far better fate, and he often spoke of Lilly becoming a governess. Although Rosie had a great deal of difficulty imagining such a fate for her daughter, she nonetheless welcomed it. Not only would Lilly be provided with an opportunity to live in a good house, but she was also likely to make a decent living, thus attracting a suitable husband.

How fortunate Lilly was to be!

Alas, such a fate was still many years away, and in the meantime, it was Rosie's job to ensure that the worst did not happen. So, she took it upon herself to educate Lilly for a few hours after school. Each afternoon upon her return, Lilly rushed home in the company of their neighbour, Mrs. Wodehouse, and her granddaughter Polly. Together, the two of them made quite a pair, laughing and giggling without a care in the world.

It warmed her heart to see such a friendship blossom between them, particularly as Polly herself was quite lonely. Having been sent to live with her grandmother by her father, who worked in the merchant navy, Polly had never known her mother. The poor creature had died in childbirth, a mere few hours after the birth of Polly.

Rosie herself had heard talk of how her father could scarcely stand to look at her.

How a few days after his wife's death, he'd arrived to deposit his daughter at his mother's doorstep before leaving right away. Mrs.

Wodehouse had been beside herself with grief and worry. Having loved her daughter-in-law quite dearly, as much as she would her own daughter, she had not hesitated to take the babe into her home.

Bless her soul.

Mrs. Wodehouse did not have much to her name.

Indeed, she scarcely had anything at all save for the room she had with her husband. In spite of their old age and the difficulty of their circumstances, neither of them had hesitated when it came to Polly. On the contrary, they did everything they could to care for her, with Mr. Wodehouse returning to his former field of employment in the shops. Mrs. Wodehouse, on the other hand, had taken up being a laundress in order to help her husband provide. Between the two of them, they did what they could to provide the little girl with a better fate.

Why, even young Polly herself, was learning how to work.

In the afternoons, after reviewing their lessons with Mrs. Wodehouse, the two of them came to Rosie with bright eyes and an eagerness to learn.

In the beginning, she had been reluctant to teach them, knowing all too well the harsh nature of a seamstress' work. Time and again, she had hesitated, loathing to push them too hard, and not wanting them to leave their childhood behind.

There was still much for them to see and experience, and Rosie did not wish to be the one to snatch that away from them. Someday, the two of them would be forced to grow up and face the harsh realities of living as a woman in the city, but for now, she wanted them to laugh, play, and soak up the warmth from the sun for as long as they could. Still, a part of her knew that it was not for her to decide their fate.

All she could do was prepare them.

And try she did.

For a few hours every day, from the time the sun was high in the sky until it set, plunging the world into darkness, she worked alongside them. Every so often, she would examine their work, pausing a little too long at their stitches before returning to her own work. Afterwards, she ushered them into the kitchen, where they helped her prepare dinner. As soon as they were done, Polly hurried off across the hall and waved at

Lilly from the doorway. Once she disappeared inside, Lilly then clung to Rosie, refusing to leave her side for an instant.

She was a dear, a kind and caring little girl with a curious mind. Rosie loved her dearly and was thankful every day that the good Lord had seen fit to bless them with her presence. Were it not for Lilly, Rosie was sure her existence would have been both dull and drab, proving to be something of a tedious chore as the days blurred together. Deciding to keep her and raise her as their own had proven to be the best decision they had ever made.

Rosie was immensely thankful her husband had seen sense.

In truth, she could not imagine Lilly in an orphanage. Whenever she tried, she pictured her curled up on a thin layer of hay in the middle of a dark and crowded room, which reeked of sweat and dirt. She saw Lilly bent over pots and pans in the kitchen, her eyes wide and sunken, and her fingers small and bony. With a shake of her head, Rosie would push the thoughts away and turn her attention to the present.

Lilly was, fortunately, theirs.

And she had not gone to the orphanage, and no one had discovered the truth of her identity. While she had been growing up, consumed with guilt, Peter had tried to learn what he could of her and her mother, but his inquires had led him to nothing. In the end, he was forced to abandon his pursuit for fear of discovery. In spite of his better judgement, Peter had grown quite attached to Lilly and often lit up in her presence, as if she was the centre of his whole world.

Bless his heart.

Lilly threw her arms around Rosie's middle and squeezed. "I love you, Mama."

With a jolt, Rosie came back to the present and found herself with a half-peeled potato in one hand and her other hand on Lilly's shoulders. She set the potato down and twisted to face her daughter, a familiar warmth blossoming in the centre of her chest. When Lilly tilted her head back to look up at her, Rosie was struck anew with gratitude.

She ran her fingers through Lilly's fine golden hair. "I love you too, my pet."

Lilly beamed and pulled back. "Mrs. Bennet said I am doing quite well in school."

Rosie's smile stretched from ear to ear. "You are a clever little girl, my dear. Your father and I are so proud."

Lilly's eyebrows drew together. "Can I be a schoolteacher like Mrs. Bennet?"

"Perhaps you can," Rosie told her with a smaller smile. "In any case, you are still too young to worry about such things."

Lilly frowned at her. "Were you not also eight when you began to work?"

"Yes, but I had to, because my father could not support all of us," Rosie replied in a quiet voice. She pushed Lilly's hair out of her face and tucked it behind her ears. "Papa had worked hard to be able to feed and clothe us."

Lilly studied her face. "Do you miss him?"

Rosie blinked. "Every day, and I miss my siblings, too."

Lilly tilted her head to the side. "Why do you not talk about them, Mama?"

"Sometimes, it is painful to talk about people who are gone," Rosie responded, her breath catching towards the end. "Although they have been gone for many years, I miss them all the time."

And she thought of them every day.

Her family was never far from her thoughts.

And at night, when she knelt down in front of the bed to pray, she thought of them fondly. She recalled the nights she had spent wedged in between her two sisters, the three of them giggling and laughing. In her mind, she still heard her two brothers arguing over the single toy they had possessed. Why, she even thought of her mother, who had been confined to her bed for years.

Yet, seeing how broken her illness had made her father and how he had retreated into himself, had broken something in young Rosie, especially when she'd discovered that he had turned to drink for comfort. For a year after her mother's death, her father only returned home in the early hours of the morning, reeking of drink and covered in his own sick. Wordlessly, she would help her sisters clean him up and put him to bed. During those times, his gaze often lingered on them wide and unflinching before he frowned. Then he would collapse onto the mattress and fall into a deep and restless sleep.

Once she was old enough to work, she had begun to learn from a kind and elderly neighbour, who had taken pity on her and her sisters. It was not long before her sisters were married off, leaving her alone with her brothers. Soon, they too left her in search of a better future for themselves. When Rosie was left to care for her father, it was Peter who had brought joy to her life.

Had it not been for him, Rosie was sure she would not have survived.

Truthfully, she would've sunk into despair and ruin, being unable to keep herself afloat any longer. Having known Peter her whole life, she had taken a liking to the kind and hard-working boy who liked to spend time with her. In the absence of her brothers and sisters, the two of them had gotten closer, and she had dared to dream of a life with him beyond the dark walls she had inhabited all her life.

Yet, war had almost taken him from her.

For months, she laid awake in bed, keeping his memory tucked closer to her heart and praying for him. While she cleaned the house, she had thought of him. In the company of her neighbour, who employed her as a seamstress, he was never far from her thoughts. As the days had gone on, her hope began to wilt away until Peter returned to her, looking far older and more haggard than the young man who had been full of life and optimism as he went off to war.

Still, she had welcomed him in. Rosie often thought of that day, and the look in Peter's eyes as he'd stared at the fire, as if he would never know peace again. She had harboured her doubts as to the man who returned, battered, hardened, and weary, but as soon as Peter's eyes held hers, she'd seen glimpses of the young man she'd loved.

Now, she could think of nowhere else she'd rather be.

Being Peter's wife was everything she'd hoped for, and more.

And having been given the chance to be a mother, two decades after marrying Peter, was more than she dared hope for. As far as she was concerned, Rosie had everything she ever wanted out of life, and the only thing that could make her happiness more complete was knowing that Lilly would be well looked after.

Giving her the chance to learn how to provide for herself was invaluable.

And it was something Rosie herself was thankful for, particularly now. Granted, Peter worked hard at the gentleman's club and brought home decent wages, but since Lilly had come into their lives, their expenses had increased.

But she was more than willing to pay for the difference.

With a shake of her head, Rosie reached for Lilly's hand and squeezed. "Let us talk of other things, my pet."

Lilly nodded and led Rosie towards the fireplace. There, she released her mother's hand, lowered herself onto the floor, and began to play with her wooden horse. Rosie watched her for a few moments before she dragged herself back to the kitchen to the potatoes that still needed to be peeled. In silence, Lilly joined her, and the two of them made quick work of the stew, before setting it to boil over the hearth.

As soon as they were done, Rosie began to cut up the bread. "Your father will be home soon."

Lilly clapped her hands together, and her green eyes lit up. "I love hearing all of Papa's stories."

"They are not just stories, my love," Rosie told her over her shoulders. "They are memories."

Lilly's eyes widened into saucers. "So, Papa really fought in a war?"

"He did."

"Is that how he hurt his leg?"

Rosie nodded. "He had fought bravely for his country."

Lilly's expression turned thoughtful. "I want to fight, too."

Rosie laughed. "You cannot, my love. Women cannot fight. You can become a governess or a seamstress or a laundress."

"Or a schoolteacher," Lilly added, jutting her chin out.

"Or a schoolteacher," Rosie agreed. "But many of the schoolteachers are nuns."

Lilly tilted her head to the side, and her eyes swept over Rosie's face. "Can I be a nun?"

"I suppose you could, if you wanted to," Rosie replied with a smile. She pulled Lilly against her and ran a hand over her face. "But you must do well at school first."

Lilly nodded eagerly. "I will."

When the door opened a second later, and Peter stepped in, Lilly shrieked with delight and launched herself at him. He caught her before they toppled to the ground and hoisted her up. As one, the two of them burst into laughter. Then he held her up underneath her arms and spun her around, her giggles filling the room. The last light of the day poured in through the window, giving them both a soft and eerie glow.

Rosie folded her arms over her chest, a small smile hovering on the edge of her lips. When Peter set her down, Lilly buried her face against his middle, and he stroked her hair. Rosie's chest swelled with emotion, and her eyes filled with tears. The two of them began to speak in hushed tones, so she turned her back on them and wandered over to the hearth.

Peter hugged Rosie from behind and pressed a kiss to the side of her head. "How are you today, my love?"

"I am well, you?"

Peter spun her around and smiled at her, his entire face looking youthful and vulnerable. "I am happy to be home."

"Will you tell me a story, Papa?" Lilly wedged herself between them and glanced back and forth between the two. "Mama told me many of your stories really happened."

Peter nodded and patted her head. "They are true, my dear."

Lilly's mouth fell open. "You are so brave, Papa."

Peter shrugged. "I did what needed to be done, my pet."

Lilly still gazed at him in awe and wonder. "But you must have been so scared."

Peter bent down and scooped her up into his arms. She sat on his lap, and he wrapped his arms around her. Wordlessly, Rosie moved around the room, filling the bowls with stew and setting loaves of bread next to them. When she was done, she brought the table in front of the fire. Together, Peter and Lilly stood up and came to sit next to her.

All through dinner, Lilly kept her eyes fixed on her father. His body turned towards her and chattering animatedly in between bites of food. Rosie watched the entire interaction with amusement, wondering if she ought not to have revealed that part of Peter's past. While it was something to be proud of, Rosie wondered if Lilly was too young to know of war and its atrocities. Yet, as she listened to Peter talk, she realized she had nothing to worry about.

Peter did not go into any gory details.

On the contrary, he spoke of the people he had met during the war, and how it felt to sleep under the stars. He went on at length, regarding the grim reality of war without scaring their daughter or making her feel as if it was something to be glorified or romanticized. By the end of it all, Lilly had fallen silent, a solemn expression on her face. After dinner, she helped Rosie tidy up before she scurried off to bed.

Peter came to stand in front of the window and studied the moonlit streets below. "She is turning into a fine young lady."

"She is," Rosie agreed, before wiping her hands on her apron. She came to stand next to her husband, and he wrapped an arm around her shoulders. "She is quite bright, too."

"Mrs. Bennet sang her praises when I saw her the other day," Peter revealed with a small smile. "Her schoolteacher believes she will go far."

Rosie nodded. "I believe so, too."

Peter twisted to face her, a furrow appearing between her brows. "Do you believe she should continue to go to school?"

Rosie blinked. "You believe she should not?"

"An education will only serve a woman to a certain extent," Peter replied with a shake of his head. "Lilly is a smart girl, but surely she must learn other skills that will be more useful."

Rosie frowned. "What if she wishes to become a governess?"

Peter blew out a breath. "You know as well as I that it will be difficult for her to become a governess given her...station."

Rosie swallowed. "I know quite well what her station is, but I do not believe she should be defined by it. I do not wish to be a bad mother."

Peter drew her into his arms and studied her face. "You are not a bad mother, not in the slightest. Forgive me, my love. I did not mean to upset you. It is only that I worry so about her."

Rosie sighed. "I worry about her, too."

And she did not wish to crush Lilly's hopes and dreams, especially at such a young age. Yet, it was not wise to encourage Lilly's pursuit of the impossible. As much as she hated to admit it, her husband was right.

It was too soon to tell for certain, but it was likely that Lilly would end up a seamstress like her mother. Considering that she was being taught how to sew, darn, and mend clothes for garment orders, it was better for her to be prepared. Unfortunately, the thought of discouraging Lilly's dreams, even if it was for the best, did not sit well with Rosie.

So, she endeavoured to give her daughter the best chance possible.

Even if it meant having to work harder.

"I am certain she will do well for herself," Peter continued after a brief pause. He pulled away from Rosie and wandered over to the fire. His handsome features were illuminated by firelight, and although his tone was quiet and full of hope, she saw the tight lines around his face, and it filled her stomach with dread.

Her husband was a good and honest man, but he carried around too much. On the rare occasions when he did speak of his job, she was led to believe that it was a fine establishment that treated him humanely. However, every now and again she heard talk of the impossible standards the staff were held to, and how there was very little room for mistakes. Rarely, if ever, were allowances made for those who did not hold to the gentleman's club's impossible standards.

Often, Rosie wondered if Peter would be better off somewhere else.

Yet, he had been recommended by a senior officer, and although it was difficult, it was dignified work, and given his injury, there were few other places that would hire him. Rosie found the entire ordeal terribly unfair, especially considering how protective she was of her husband, but she knew he could handle himself.

Having worked there for the last twenty years, Peter knew how to keep to himself, and he had made himself indispensable to his employers. So much so, that he was often tasked with hiring new employees in order to better serve the establishment. Over the years, many had come and gone, for a wide array of reasons, but Peter still stood tall and steadfast.

She was immensely proud of her husband.

But her heart ached for him, and the dreams he too was forced to cast aside. Although the two of them had long since made their peace with their fate, having vowed to make the most of their situation, now and again, she found herself wondering what would've become of her if Peter had not returned. Or if he had not gone off to war to begin with.

Would the Lord have given them a better life?

Would Lilly have come into their lives at all?

With a little more force than necessary, she shoved the thought aside and turned her attention to her husband. She walked over to him and took his hand in hers. After a while, he squeezed her hand and twisted his head to look at her, a strange glint in his eyes.

"Do you regret marrying me?"

"Of course not. Why would I regret marrying you?"

Peter's expression grew dismayed. "I have done my best to provide you with a good life, Rosie, and I know I promised you so much more. I am sorry I have not been able to live up to the promise."

Rosie took both of her husband's hands in her and squeezed. "You have nothing to apologize for, my love. We have made a good life together."

Peter lowered his head. "I wish I could give you and Lilly more. The two of you deserve so much better."

"You have already given us so much." Rosie pulled him against her and watched the shadows dance along the walls. "The three of us have each other, and we are happy together. What more could we possibly want?"

Peter drew back to study her face. "Do you truly believe so?"

"I do." Rosie kissed his forehead before drawing away. "You have no reason to believe such things. You are a good man, Peter Chalmers, and I am lucky to be your wife. And we are both fortunate that we have been blessed with Lilly."

Peter clasped his hands behind his back. "Sometimes I worry she will be taken away from us. Do you ever wonder if someone is looking for her?"

Rosie paused and released a deep breath. "I do, but Lilly is our daughter. For the past few years, we are the ones who have raised her, fed her, and clothed her."

"She is our daughter," Peter agreed. "But I do believe that someday, we ought to tell her the truth about the circumstances regarding how she came to be here."

Rosie's stomach dipped. "We will, but let us not speak of such things now. Such a day is a good long while away."

Peter exhaled. "You are right. I cannot help but worry about such things. But I know that we are in the good Lord's hands."

Rosie nodded and bowed her head.

Sometime later, when the two of them retired for the evening, Lilly was already fast asleep, her hands tucked underneath her chin, and her body curled in on itself. Rosie changed into her nightgown and stood before her daughter, committing every single feature to memory.

Oh, how she wanted to protect her from the world.

But she also wanted Lilly to have a life so full of joy and adventure. With bated breath, she ran her hands over Lilly's face and waited. When Lilly smiled in her sleep, Rosie's stomach tightened in response. She bent down and pressed a kiss to her daughter's forehead. Then she knelt down by the edge of the bed and clasped her hands together in a quick prayer.

As soon as she was done, she rose to her feet and blew out the candle, casting the room into darkness. On the other side of her, the bed creaked and groaned underneath Peter's weight. When he pulled her to him, she sighed and melted against his touch.

Lord have mercy and deliver us from evil.

Chapter Three

Ten years later…

"You cannot be serious." Lilly gave a slight shake of her head, and her eyebrows drew together in concentration. "You know as well as I that we cannot take on anymore work."

Polly placed both hands on her hips and blew on a wayward strand of brown hair. "Why ever not?"

Lilly set the dress down and glanced up at her friend. "Because we already have more clients than we know what to do with, especially now that we have taken on Mama's."

Polly frowned. "But we can do more."

"The results would not be as good," Lilly protested. She stood up and stretched her arms over her head. "We are already doing quite well, Poll. There is no need to push our luck."

Particularly not when they had gotten this lucky.

Not only had the two of them been working as seamstresses since they were little, but had also developed quite a reputation for themselves at the tender ages of eighteen. While the two of them were similar in age, they could not have been more different in temperament or personality. Where Lilly was quiet, reserved and kept to herself, Polly had the tendency to be wild and outspoken, finding herself in trouble more times than she cared to admit.

Together, the two of them made an unlikely pair, but Lilly could not imagine a better friend to be by her side. Since she had come to live with the Chalmers, Polly had been her faithful companion and confidant, and now that the two of them were older and capable of working, they were still as close as ever.

Lilly could think of no one she liked better.

Save for the Chalmers, who had raised her as their own.

She had so few memories of her time before the Chalmers, and many of them were of dark, damp rooms and hunger gnawing on the insides of her stomach. Now and again, a woman's face appeared in her memory, peering intently at her, but she could not quite make out her features. Try as she might, Lilly could not seem to bring her into focus, no matter how badly she wished it.

And it frustrated her to no end.

All she wanted was to see her face!

Surely it was not too much to ask to be able to see the face of the woman who had birthed her and cared for her during the first few years of her life. Lilly remembered a smooth and lilting voice, and soft skin. Beyond that, there was little else she remembered, and it often kept her up at night.

She tossed and turned on her mattress by the fireplace while her parents slept in the next room. Although she did not mean to be ungrateful, time and again she wondered as to the strange circumstances that had brought her to the city. In all of her memories, she could not seem to recall much beyond clear blue skies and fields of grass stretched as far as the eye could see.

How maddening it all was!

Had her birth mother lived in the country?

Over the years, Lilly had broached the subject with Rosie, but her mother had been reluctant to discuss the matter. Once, Rosie had gone into great detail about the night they had found Lilly, and the sorry state of her, even going so far as to mention the death of her mother, Rosie's sister.

All of the neighbours and Lilly herself were told the same tragic story, and the mysterious circumstances surrounding Lilly's mother's death. But that night was seldom mentioned again, and in spite of her best efforts, it was unlikely to be discussed ever again.

Lilly sensed it was too painful for Rosie.

And Peter, too.

Yet, she did not have the heart to push them any further than she already had. Forcing them to relieve what was, doubtless, an incredibly painful memory for them made no sense. Especially when they had never let her want for anything. Not only had they provided her with a good education, particularly for a woman of her social standing, but they'd also done their best to keep her in school until she could no longer attend classes. Lilly had done quite well as a student, and her schoolteacher, who had been with her for several years, had sung Lilly's praises and had looked quite beside herself with grief when Lilly had been forced to leave.

It had been Mrs. Bennet's great hope that Lilly would replace her.

For a time, Lilly had dreamt of the same thing.

Until Rosie had fallen ill, and Lilly was forced to help tend to her.

While Peter still kept a decent number of hours at the gentleman's club, without Rosie's wages, things had been difficult. Fortunately, it had not taken long for Lilly to take up the mantel, and with Polly's help, the two of them had split Rosie's clientele among them. Then they had both amassed clients of their own coming from far and wide in order to seek out their services.

Lilly was filled with pride at their accomplishments.

In spite of the odds stacked against them, the two of them had risen above it and proven themselves to be worthy. Furthermore, with their combined wages, Lilly and Polly were able to support the Wodehouses and the Chalmers, and Lilly prayed they would be able to do so well into their old age. By the looks of things, it would not be much longer until Peter himself would be unable to work.

She knew her father took great pride in working at the gentleman's club, the establishment that had filled her imagination for a great many years, but she also knew that it was only a matter of time before he was asked to leave. The club prided itself on being able to cater to their clients and maintain a certain standard of service. Given Peter's old age and his injury, it wouldn't be long before he could no longer maintain either. Until then, she prayed her father was able to do his job with both dignity and grace.

Lord, watch over my father, and please see to it that he is not treated with unkindness and disrespect.

"….are you even listening to me?"

Lilly blinked, and she was brought back to the present with a jolt. "What?"

Polly sighed and placed both hands on her hips, her dark eyes narrowing at Lilly. "You ought to listen more, Lilly, and get your head out of the clouds. It is not becoming of a young lady to daydream so often."

Lilly frowned. "I was not daydreaming. I was only thinking of the circumstances that brought me here."

"Under the Chalmers roof? I remember your poor mother being quite beside herself. The day you came into their lives, something changed for the Chalmers. I do not think they have ever been so happy."

Guilt churned in her stomach. "Surely I did not make that much of a difference."

"I have heard my grandmother discussing the matter with my grandfather," Polly continued after a quick look around the room. She moved closer to Lilly and lowered her voice. "For years the Chalmers had hoped for a child only to be told they could not have any of their own."

"How awful," Lilly muttered, her stomach giving another twinge. "It is fortunate that I came to live with him."

Polly nodded. "Your mother's sister was given a good and honourable burial."

Lilly studied Polly's face. "You should not be eavesdropping, Pol. You know how much your grandmother detests such behaviour."

Polly tossed her head back and grinned. "She does not know that I am behaving in an un-lady like fashion. She would be most displeased if she knew."

"You must stop, then."

"I cannot," Polly replied with a brighter smile. "Oh, Lil. There is far too much to experience and to see to bother with propriety and social niceties."

A groan spilled out into the sitting room. Lilly glanced over her shoulders, then she exchanged a quick look with Polly. She paused to drape the dress over the back of the chair before hurrying into her mother's room. Rosie sat propped up against the pillow, thin greying hair falling in waves around her shoulders, and in a heavy cream-colored gown that did little to hide her frail form.

Old age had not been kind to her mother.

Years of tending to dresses and trying to produce the best version possible had caught up to her. Now, Rosie could scarcely lift her arm without doubling over in pain. Several doctors had been to visit her, and they had all declared the same thing. Unfortunately, her mother could no longer tend to her own work, much less that of her house. Offering to take on her clientele had come as a relief to Rosie, but she had still seen the guilt in her mother's eyes.

Rosie's eyes fluttered open as soon as Lilly closed the door, and she smiled. "You needn't mind me, my pet. I am certain there is much work to tend to."

Lilly shook her head and crept forward. After adjusting her pillow, Lilly reached for the cup of water and held it up to Rosie's lips. Rosie's cracked lips moved slowly and trembled, leaving her incapable of taking more than a few sips of water. When she was done, she leaned back and sank against the mattress, drawing the cover up to her chin.

Wordlessly, Lilly set the cup down and folded her arms over her chest. "You must try to drink, Mama."

"I do," Rosie protested in a weak voice. "And you have become quite an accomplished cook, my dear. I am so proud."

"You have taught me everything," Lilly pointed out, her breath catching towards the end. "And now it is your turn to rest."

Rosie peered at her, hazel eyes full of emotion. "I am so proud of the young woman you are becoming. Truly, I cannot think of a blessing greater than being your mother."

Lilly's own eyes filled with tears. "Every day, I am thankful that you and Papa took me in."

Rosie cleared her throat. "We could not have turned you away. You were such a small and frail thing, and you were in need of us. As much as we were in need of you."

Lilly's throat turned dry. "Mama, I wish to know—"

Rosie sank further against the mattress and squeezed her eyes shut. "I am quite tired. I should very much like to rest now."

Lilly swallowed. "Alright, mama. We will talk later."

As soon as her mother's breathing evened out, Lilly tiptoed out of the room. Out in the hallway, Lilly brought her head to a rest against the wall and blew out a deep breath. Over, and over, she turned the matter over in her head, but the more she did, the guiltier she felt. The Chalmers had been under no obligation to take her in, but they had opened their doors and hearts to her, and in return, she loved them fiercely with all of her might.

As far as she was concerned, they were the only parents she needed or had ever known.

Truthfully, she would not have it any other way, but every so often, she found herself wondering about her own birth parents and what had become of her father. Having perished on the journey to the city, it had not taken much persuading from Lilly to learn what had become of her mother. Her father, on the other hand, was a different matter altogether.

Was he still alive?

Had he cast her out because he did not want her?

Or because he could not care for her in the way she needed?

Lilly stiffened and pushed herself away from the wall. Quietly, she walked back into the sitting room and took up her seat next to the fire. Over the next few hours, she half listened to Polly, who rambled on and on about her adventures, and the great plans she had for herself, and the other half continued to spin and race in circles, fearful of what would happen if she confronted Peter.

Do not be foolish, Lilly. The Chalmers are still family, and they have done right by you in all the ways that count. Continuing to pursue this is not only folly, but it is also deeply hurtful.

Resolved to put the matter out of her mind once and for all, Lilly then turned her attention to Polly, and the two of them spent hours working and discussing a wide array of topics. When the sun began to dip below the horizon, her father returned, briefly darkening the doorway before he stepped in. She rose to greet him, and he pulled her into a deep hug. Later, the two of them sat down to dinner, with Rosie in between them, propped up against her pillow.

It was a quiet and sombre affair, and Lilly was all too glad to finish, so she could retire to the sitting room and the book she left behind. That night, she sat by the fire, reading until her eyes stung, and her limbs grey heavy. With a deep yawn and a sigh, she had forced herself to close the book and crawl onto the mattress.

That night, Lilly fell into a deep and dreamless sleep.

***

"I believe that is them." Lilly rose to her feet and pushed the window open, allowing a warm breeze smelling of wildflowers to pour in. She inhaled and ran her hands along the front of her dress, resisting the urge to tuck her hair behind her ears.

Mrs. Bloom was one of their most important clients.

Often, she came to them in the company of her lady's maid, who served as her eyes, given that the old lady had lost all of her vision. Whenever she visited, Lilly and Polly took it upon themselves to clear the room of anything harmful, in order to ensure Mrs. Bloom had a successful and harmless visit.

Mrs. Bloom herself was a kind and sharp old woman with streaks of silver in her dark hair, milky white brown eyes, and a keen sense of fashion, even at her old age. Many times, Lilly had to pause and admire their creation tailored according to Mrs. Bloom's exact modifications.

In her heyday, Mrs. Bloom must've been quite the bell of the ball. Whenever Lilly imagined such things, she allowed her flights of fancy a few moments before reeling them back in. Today was no exception.

Except when the door opened, and Mrs. Bloom came in, she was not accompanied by her short and dark-haired lady's maid, who always donned a polite smile on her face. Instead, she was accompanied by a young, fashionably dressed woman in a lavender dress with golden hair and emerald eyes.

Lilly tried not to stare at her. "Good morning, Mrs. Bloom."

"Good morning," Mrs. Bloom replied, turning the full force of her gaze on Lilly. "How is your aunt today, Miss Chalmer?"

"She is faring better, Mrs. Bloom," Lilly replied with a warm smile. "Thank you for your kind inquiry."

Mrs. Bloom waved her hand away. Then her hand darted out and closed around the young woman's elbow. "This is my granddaughter. Miss Shelly Bloom."

Lilly inclined her head in the blonde's direction. "How do you do, Miss Bloom?"

Shelly gave her a warm smile and led her grandmother towards the chair set up in the centre of the room. "I have heard a great deal about your establishment, Miss Chalmer, and of the work the two of you do."

Polly flushed. "How kind of you, Miss Bloom. We do our best for our clients."

Shelly helped her grandmother sit down and adjusted the folds of her dress around the chair. "I have heard many speak highly of your skills. Is it only the two of you?"

Lilly nodded. "Yes, Miss."

Shelly straightened her back and spun around to face them with a bright smile. "I think it is wonderful how two young, accomplished ladies such as yourself have done so well for themselves and their families."

Mrs. Bloom murmured her agreement.

Wordlessly, Polly walked over to Mrs. Bloom and placed a hand on her arm. The old woman rose to her feet and lifted her chin up. In silence, Lilly and Polly moved around each other, working together to make sure the measurements were in order. While they were working, they made polite conversation with Shelly, who was all too happy to engage in conversation with young women who were similar in age to her.

Little by little, she revealed that she was visiting her grandmother while her parents were on business. Her father, Simon Bloom, a well-to-do member of the landed gentry, typically resided in the countryside along with his family. However, they did make frequent trips to the city in order to take up residence in their London townhouse and see to any affairs that needed their attention. Meanwhile, Shelly's mother, Celia Bloom, was the daughter of a family with ties to a duke and was currently seeing to the affairs of the country house by making all the necessary purchases.

Lilly could scarcely believe such an existence was possible.

And the more Shelly described certain aspects of her life, the more wistful Lilly became, until she imagined herself sitting on top of a hill overlooking fields of grass, and a cosy little cottage in the centre. When she blinked, the image was gone, and she found herself staring at the hem of the dark coloured dress Mrs. Bloom had requested. With a shake of her head, Lilly pushed away all such thoughts and returned to the work at hand.

It would not do to allow herself to get caught up in such fanciful daydreams, particularly not when she knew what to expect out of life. A woman such as herself was expected to work until she found a husband of a similar station. Afterwards, she was to continue to work and tend to the house. Someday, Lilly was going to have children of her own and teach them how to mend and sew clothing.

And on and on, the cycle would go.

Most days, Lilly was grateful, having seen first-hand many of the less fortunate who lived in the dark alleys and lurked on the streets of the city. Often, when she and Polly were out on walks, venturing towards the city's markets and stalls, she saw them with their sunken faces and empty eyes, and it sent a shiver racing up and down her spine. As hard as she tried to ignore the ominous feeling that lingered with her, it often took days before she could set herself to rights again.

Those poor unfortunate souls.

"Forgive me, Miss Bloom," Polly began in a strange voice. "But you look quite familiar."

"What can you mean?"

Polly studied Shelly's face, then looked over at Lilly, who was bent over the table, a furrow between her brows. When she glanced up, she saw Polly's eyes widen, and a myriad of emotions dance across her face.

"How remarkable."

Lilly frowned. "What are you talking about?"

Rosie wandered into the room and sucked in a harsh breath when she saw Shelly. She glanced over at Lilly, and she lingered a little too long, prompting her daughter to rise to her feet.

"Mama, you should be resting."

"I am feeling better today," Rosie replied in a faint voice. "And I wished to make sure you were not in need of my assistance."

"They are both doing quite well, Mrs. Chalmer," Mrs. Bloom assured her with a small smile. "Your clients are in excellent and quite capable hands."

Rosie looked over at Mrs. Bloom and blinked. "Thank you, Mrs. Bloom. How very kind of you."

"Mrs. Chalmer." Polly came to stand beside Lilly and took her hand. "Does Lilly not look exactly like Miss Bloom?"

"Miss Bloom?"

"This is Ms. Shelly Bloom," Polly clarified. "Mrs. Bloom's granddaughter."

Rosie cleared her throat. "I see. It is a pleasure to meet you, Miss Bloom."

Lilly glanced over at Shelly and frowned. "There is a resemblance, but I daresay you are all reading too much into it."

Shelly covered the distance between them and came to a stop a few feet away. For a while, the two of them studied each other, while Lilly's heart thudded against her chest. Granted, the resemblance was uncanny, and it left Lilly with knots in her stomach, but she was certain it was merely a strange and eerie coincidence. Shelly Bloom was, after all, the daughter of gentry and not only had she been brought up as such, but she was also in possession of a keen and sharp mind.

As evidenced by her mannerisms and the way she spoke.

"I do favour my father's looks," Shelly revealed with a quick glance around the room. Her eyes lingered on her grandmother, and a thoughtful expression crossed her face. "It is a pity I did not take more after mother."

Mrs. Bloom waved her comment away. "Nonsense, my dear. You are the best of the both of them."

Lilly's eyes settled on Mrs. Bloom, who was bathed in a soft halo of yellow light. With a shake of her head, she sat back down and returned to her work. Still, her mother, Polly and Shelly discussed the matter in hushed tones, often gesturing to Lilly who was adamant on ignoring all of them.

The resemblance did not mean anything at all.

And the sooner everyone stopped fussing over it, the better it would be for all of them.

***

"Papa."

Simon Bloom set down his newspaper and smiled at his daughter, who lingered in the doorway to his study. When he beckoned her forward, she stepped in and glanced around at the shelves upon shelves of books pressed against the door and came to a stop a few feet away from his desk. He sat up straighter and linked his fingers together.

"What is it, my pet?"

"I'm sorry to disturb you, Papa." Shelly tucked her hair behind her ears and stood up straighter. "I wanted to see how you were feeling."

"I am far better, my dear." Simon motioned to the chair opposite him, and Shelly sank gratefully into it, rearranging the folds of her green dress, so it was settled around her. "I have had a most productive day."

Shelly smiled at him. "I am most glad to hear it."

"And you? Did you enjoy accompanying your grandmother to the seamstress?"

A strange look settled across his daughter's features. "Quite, but it was the most peculiar thing. Grandma's seamstress is no longer capable of tending to her needs, so it was her daughter who helped us."

Simon raised an eyebrow. "Why is that peculiar? Many young ladies of a different station are forced to work in order to help provide for the family."

Shelly nodded. "I know, Papa, but what is unusual is the young lady in question."

Simon frowned and unlinked his fingers. "Was she rude or unhelpful?"

Shelly shook her head, a lock of hair falling over her eyes. "Not at all, Papa. On the contrary, I found Ms. Chalmer to be quite helpful and accommodating. As was Ms. Wodehouse. What the two of them have managed to accomplish is quite impressive."

Simon blinked. "So, what is the issue?"

"She looks like me," Shelly blurted out, leaning forward and holding his gaze. "It was a little unnerving at first, but the more I studied her features, the more of myself I saw. Even her mother and Ms. Wodehouse made the same observation."

Simon's stomach dropped. "Are you certain?"

Shelly nodded slowly. "I am quite certain, Papa. What a strange thing it was to see."

Abruptly, Simon rose to his feet and stepped out from behind the desk. "I have some business to tend to."

"Now?"

"Yes, I had quite forgotten." Simon bent down to place a kiss on top of her head. "Do forgive me, my dear. I shall be back as soon as I can."

With that, he hurried out of the study and into the hallway. As soon as he reached the front door, he wrenched it open, and his valet scurried over with his coat and hat. Wordlessly, Simon donned them and issued a series of orders, his feet tapping impatiently against the floor.

By the time the coachmen brought the carriage around, Simon was filled with impatience and a strange sense of euphoria. "Take me to the seamstress' residence at once."

"Yes, sir." The coachmen dipped his head and waited for Simon to settle inside the carriage. As soon as he did, the carriage jostled and lurched forward. His hands clenched into fists at his side, and he brought his head to a rest against the glass, barely able to hear past the pounding of his own heart.

Could it be?

After twenty years of searching and wondering, was he finally about to have the answers he had so desperately yearned for? Had spent many sleepless nights imagining? Simon could not say for certain. All he knew was that he had to get to the seamstress' house so he could gaze upon the young lady in question and know for certain.

Sometime later, the coachmen pulled up outside the same address Simon himself had visited some days before. He didn't wait for the door to open before he flew out. At the top of the stairs, he drew to a halt and straightened his back. He ran a hand over his face and swallowed.

Would she know who he was?

Before he could change his mind, Simon brought his hand up and rapped on the door. After a few moments, he heard a shuffle, and the door creaked open. A young woman with a small nose, almond shaped green eyes and golden hair opened the door. She peered at him and frowned.

"Can I help you?"

"Are you Ms. Lilly Chalmer?"

She stood up straighter, and a furrow appeared between her brows. "I am."

Simon took off his hat and tucked it underneath his arm. "I am Simon Bloom."

"Mr. Bloom." Lilly pulled the door open and took a step back. "Forgive me. I was not aware that you were to be stopping by today. I am afraid we have not finished Mrs. Bloom's clothing yet."

"It is quite alright."

A man appeared behind her, with streaks of silver in his hair, and a weathered face. He placed a hand on Lilly's shoulders and eyed Simon wearily. "Can we help you?"

"Papa. This is Mr. Bloom. He is Mrs. Bloom's son." She switched her gaze back to Simon, and a jolt went through him when she smiled. Suddenly, it was as if he was looking at Penelope all over again, young and unaffected by time. The knots in his stomach tightened, and it took all his self-control not to pull Lilly to him.

"I am sorry for the intrusion," Simon began, sweat forming on the back of his neck. "I will send someone for the dress later."

With that, he spun on his heels and hurried back outside. Out on the streets, he tilted his head back and saw Lilly come to the window. When she turned her head to the side, talking to someone he could not see, he could not stop staring at her.

There was no mistaking whose daughter she was.

She looked exactly the same as Penelope had all those years ago, and he found himself yearning for the love of his life again, as he often did. Seeing Lilly alive and well filled him with a strange sense of hope and an ache in his chest for all that she did not know. Simon willed himself to move, to return to the townhouse, and to the family that awaited him, but he could not.

Not when he had finally found her.

So, he stood there, gazing upon her for a while longer and noticing all the little similarities between Lilly and the woman who had captured his heart twenty years earlier. Although she had been gone for longer than he knew her, she had never left him, and Penelope Wickham, daughter of a widowed vicar, would always be the love of his life.

Even if theirs had been a tragic love affair.

Chapter Four

Twenty years prior

Simon Bloom had never known the carefree life that many young men his age lead.

Instead of being allowed to act his age and discover all the world had to offer for a man of his wealth and opportunity, he was forced to tend to his father's sprawling estate. Having died two years prior, Simon had been left with the responsibility sitting squarely on his shoulders.

The household staff and the tenant farmers turned to him, and it was only with his mother's help, and by the grace of God, that he was able to do it all. Granted, his father had raised him as his only son and heir to one day take over the estate, but neither of them had expected the late Mr. Bloom to perish so suddenly and without a warning.

Why, Simon himself had expected his father, being the strong and proud man that he was to live to a ripe old age, and rule over the Bloom estate with an iron fist from the shadows. Truthfully, it had given Simon a great deal of comfort, given that he himself felt unequipped to handle such an affair.

Yet fate was a cruel and often harsh mistress.

Mr. Bloom had died on a warm summer's day, having collapsed while tending to some business in his study. It was Simon who had happened upon him, having returned from a ride around the estate with his mother for company. Together, the two of them had cried out for help and rushed to aid the gasping and flailing patriarch of the Bloom family. A doctor was sent over, but some hours later, when the sun was high in the sky, and set against a backdrop of clear blue skies, Robert Bloom had drawn his last breath. His mother had been beside herself with grief, and it had taken everything within him to pry her away from her husband's bedside.

For weeks, his mother would not leave her room and scarcely spoke to anyone. While he tended to his father's affairs and saw to the affairs of the estate, his mother grieved and sunk further and further into herself. At the tender age of eighteen, Simon found himself with the weight of the world on his shoulders, and a desolate and inconsolable mother.

Those days had not been easy.

In the end, it was the arrival of the vicar two years after the death of his father, and his mild manner and soft-spoken daughter that led him back into the light. Simon had taken one look at the daughter with her dark hair, small nose, and almond-shaped eyes, and he hadn't been able to look away. And when she blushed prettily, he had forced his attention back to his valet, who had stood quiet the entire time.

From that day on, Simon found excuses to be at the vicar's, often spending long hours in their company in the hopes of seeing Penelope. Through their visits, Simon came to learn that the vicar had lost his wife some years back and had been tasked with raising his daughter alone. While she did not say much during his visits, Simon could tell that she was a strong and kind woman who doted on her father and was willing to dedicate her entire life to him.

It made him like her all the more.

He had never come across such kindness and warmth before.

So, he began to spend more and more time at the vicarage, dividing his attention between the estate and Penelope. Little by little, she began to confide in him, to blossom before his very eyes, and he found himself completely enthralled by her. Whatever spell she had cast, Simon was willing to follow her anywhere, and he found himself suddenly grateful that his mother had so little interest in him and his life.

Anne Bloom would not approve of his feelings.

Nor would she approve of his dalliance with the vicar's daughter, of all people.

Not only was Simon the heir to the estate, but he was also expected to marry well, bringing honour and fortune to the family, and expanding their connections. As far as his mother was concerned, marriage was a business contract, not to be entered into lightly and only to be undertaken when he was sure of the success it would yield.

Talking to her of his burgeoning feelings would not do.

On the contrary, it would only cause problems for the vicar and Penelope, and the last thing he wanted, particularly when they had opened their doors to him, was to bring problems to their doorstep. For months, Simon paid them weekly visits, often twice a week, and his visits grew lengthier. The three of them grew accustomed to each other, and Simon found comfort and solace, the likes of which were not available to him on the Bloom Estate.

So it was that Simon found himself seeking shelter under their roof one stormy autumn evening. Through the windows, he had watched as the sky turned grey and began to pour. He heard the rise and fall of conversation through the walls, but he paid it no mind, his mind instead wandering to how best to make his way back to the estate. Unfortunately, the more time that went on, the worse the weather became until it became clear that Simon would be forced to stay at the vicarage.

His heart swelled at the thought of being in such close proximity to Penelope for an extended period of time. The vicar welcomed him with a bright smile and kind eyes and insisted that Simon take his own room while he stayed with Penelope in her room. That night, Simon paced from end of the room to the next, unable to stomach the thought of being so close to Penelope, yet unable to reach for her. Eventually, he made his way outside for a glass of water and froze in the middle of the hallway.

Penelope wore a nightgown that fell down to her knees, her dark hair falling in loose waves around her shoulders. When he glanced up at her mouth, he saw the surprise written there and fell silent. Wordlessly, she handed him the glass of water and brushed past him. Lightning lit up the hallway and thunder boomed in the distance, driving Penelope closer to him.

As soon as her hand brushed against his, he was lost.

Sometime later, by the light of the moon that shone into the Vicar's room, Simon found himself undressing Penelope. Now and again, they tried to stop, with Penelope murmuring her concerns, but when the tide of emotion grew to be too great, they fell silent and instead turned to each other for comfort. He took her to bed and spent hours marvelling at Penelope and the emotions she stirred within him.

Two days later, Simon was forced to return to the estate.

Yet, the thought of Penelope and the feel of her lingered with him. For days after he could smell her on him, and he often thought of her with a smile, causing the quickening of his pulse. Although it took him a while to come up with an excuse to visit the vicarage once more, particularly with his mother taking a renewed interest in him and his affairs, he eventually made it there.

Only to find that the vicar had fallen ill again.

A few months prior, he had been struck by some unknown illness, and Penelope had confided in Simon that she had been doing her best to care for him. While his health had improved in the time since then, the vicar had not regained his strength. Unfortunately, when Simon set eyes on him and saw the ashen colour on his face and the strain in his voice, his heart broke for Penelope.

Still, she seemed to take a great deal of comfort in his visits, so he endeavoured to stop by as often as he could. When the estate did not require his attention, he rode out to them, bringing with him fruit and vegetables to bolster the vicar's strength. Already, he knew that many in the country were talking of him and his interest in the vicar and his daughter, but he could not bring himself to care.

Propriety be damned.

Alas, a fortnight later, unable to fight his illness any longer, the vicar succumbed and drew his last breath with Penelope and Simon in his presence. The vicar was laid to rest, and Penelope withdrew into herself, turning Simon away as she did. A week later, when he went to visit her, Penelope sat with him by the fireplace, her features pale and withdrawn.

"I am to leave the country in a few days," Penelope whispered, refusing to meet his gaze. "I have written to several people, and I have heard back regarding a job post nearer to London."

Simon swallowed. "What will you do?"

"I am to be a governess," Penelope replied with a small smile. "Papa would have been proud, and I will be making decent wages."

Simon cleared his throat. "I am glad to hear it."

Penelope stared at him. "Are you?"

Simon nodded and blew out a breath. "I do not know how I shall manage without you, but I shall try."

Penelope's eyes filled with tears. "I wish I did not have to leave you."

"I will write to you," Simon promised, pausing to take her hands in his. They were cold and frail against his own, but he didn't care. "I will write to you all the time, Pen. And I will come and see you as often as I can."

Wordlessly, he drew her into his arms and held her as she wept.

***

Three weeks after she took up her post at the grand country estate of the Devons' to care two children, true to his word, Simon had come to visit her. She had been beside herself with joy, and happy to find that their feelings for each other were as strong as ever. Although he was only able to stay for two days, she spent every free moment she could spare in his company.

Penelope longed for the day when she was to be well and truly his.

For now, she was content to steal away moments with him whenever possible. Some weeks later, when Penelope realized she was with child, she wrote to him, with tears in her eyes and hope in her heart. With shaky hands, she had sent the letter and eagerly awaited his response.

Unfortunately, no response came.

Resolved, Penelope wrote to him once more, begging for him to come and see her. When her second letter went unanswered, Penelope wrote to him a final time, longing for the man who had promised to love and cherish her.

Her Simon was lost to her forever.

For weeks, she wandered around the estate, lonely and desolate. Even the thought of carrying his child brought no comfort. If anything, it made her even more miserable, as did the realization that as soon as she was found out, she would be cast out onto the street. It did not matter that she had grown to care for the Devon children, nor they for her. Sure enough, on a cold winter morning, where there was nary a cloud in sight, Mrs. Devon happened on her and sent her packing.

Given that she had nowhere to go and no family to support her with her dear father having been laid to rest some months earlier, Penelope gathered her few meagre belongings and found herself on the street. For days, she wandered the country in search of employment and shelter.

Alas, many who crossed her path were not kind.

Before she knew what she was doing, Penelope found herself standing in front of the Bloom country estate. She placed both hands around the wrought-iron gates and stared. From a distance, the estate looked as majestic and beautiful as she had remembered, with its brick walls and a sprawling fountain a few feet away from the main door. As soon as the doors opened, her pulse quickened, and she squinted into the light.

She saw the back of his head first, and when he turned, her breath caught in her throat. Penelope opened her mouth, but the words would not come. From where he was standing, Simon was not going to be able to see her. Given that he had not responded to her letters, she knew it was not wise of her to be there. Yet, she could not bring herself to move, even when Simon had turned and walked away. Penelope studied the muscles of his back, and her throat turned dry. Then Mrs. Bloom came out, a solemn expression on her face.

Penelope's heart began to thud against her chest when Simon's mother saw her. She straightened her back and glided towards her, her black dress rustling behind her. Mrs. Bloom stood up straighter, clasped her hands behind her back, and fixed her dark and cruel eyes on Penelope.

"You are not welcome here," Mrs. Bloom said in a clear voice. "You are not to set foot here ever again."

Penelope wrapped an arm around her stomach and swallowed. "Please. I must speak with Si— Mr. Bloom."

Mrs. Bloom narrowed her eyes at Penelope. "He does not wish to speak with you."

Penelope sucked in a harsh breath. "So, he has received my letters?"

Mrs. Bloom lifted her chin up. "He has, and he has made it clear that he does not wish to contain your *acquaintance*."

Penelope's mouth caught on a sob. "Mrs. Bloom, I beg of you. Please ask your son to reconsider. I have been cast out of my old posting with no references, and I have nowhere else to go."

Mrs. Bloom's eyes fell to her stomach. "How dare you ask such a thing of me? I know the nature of your condition, and so does my son. He wants nothing to do with you, or the creature growing inside of you."

Penelope took a step back and another. The back of her eyes burned. "But it is his child, too. Surely—"

"Silence," Mrs. Bloom snapped, her eyes growing wide and furious. "You will not speak of my son and drag his name through the mud in such a manner. I will not allow it."

"I—"

"How could you think my son would want anything to do with you? You were merely a plaything, a passing amusement."

Penelope's stomach dropped. "It cannot be."

Mrs. Bloom's lips twisted into a sneer. "It is, and the sooner you come to terms with it, the better it will be for all of us."

Penelope fell silent.

What was she to do now?

Now that her Simon had abandoned her, what was to become of her? What was to become of her child?

Although she could scarcely believe it, she had to come to terms with the fact that Simon no longer wanted anything to do with her. Considering he had not responded to her letters and now refused to see her, she could only assume he had grown tired of her. With a shake of her head, she began to wonder if every word spoken, every promise made, was little more than a lie.

Designed to seduce her.

Since she was now a fallen woman, Simon's interested had waned. She swallowed past the lump in her throat and hugged her stomach. "What am I to do?"

"That is no concern of mine," Mrs. Bloom told her coldly. "Simon has made it clear that he wants nothing to do with a wanton and wayward woman such as yourself."

Penelope flinched. "I did not mean to—"

Mrs. Bloom held up a hand. "Your excuses do not interest me. If I ever see you near this property again, I shall be forced to have the constable take you."

Penelope paled. "Mrs. Bloom. Have mercy. I beg of you."

Mrs. Bloom pointed over Penelope's shoulder and glared. "Take your belongings and go before I call out for help."

Penelope scrambled backwards, her eyes never leaving the Bloom matriarch's face. When she was far enough away, and Mrs. Bloom was little more than a speck, the older woman spun on her heels and marched back into the house. For a few moments, Penelope watched her until the knots in her stomach made her chest tighten. She bent over and sucked in several harsh breaths, but she could scarcely breathe.

Oh, Penelope. What have you done? You should never have trusted Simon or his sweet words and kind smile. Look what has befallen you now, and your poor child.

With tears streaming down her cheeks, she gathered up the folds of her dress and fled. She could scarcely make out her surroundings, much less where she was going, only that she needed to leave the Bloom estate and get as far away as possible. As soon as she was sure there was enough space between her and their wretched estate, she leaned against a tree by the side of the road and slumped to the floor.

Then she brought her knees up to her chest and wept.

Each sob and each hiccough reverberated through her head and her body until she was weak with hunger and exhaustion. Slowly, she lifted her head up and glanced at the empty road stretched out before her. Now and again, a wagon passed by, kicking up dirt and gravel. For the most part, no one saw her. So much so that she began to wonder if she had gone invisible, the weight of her grief dragging her down.

Eventually, a young woman and her father stopped, offering her a blanket and bread. She stammered out her gratitude, and when the woman patted her on the back, the tears came again, swiftly this time. Once they died down, the young woman told her of a village nearby that had a washerwoman in search of a helper. Her eyes had travelled over Penelope as she said this, lingering over her stomach. Penelope hid her hand and gave the woman a weak but grateful smile.

On the seventh day, when she was weak and nearly blind with hunger, she stumbled into the small village nearby the city. There, she made the acquaintance of the kindly washerwoman whose husband had taken ill some years back and perished not long after. Mrs. Dashwood, who had bright eyes and a caring disposition, took pity on Penelope, particularly in her fragile condition, and offered her a room and food in exchange for her help.

That night, Penelope had cried in relief.

Not only had the washerwoman been kind enough to employ her, but she also kept an eye on Penelope, ensuring that she and the baby were faring well. So, the days turned into weeks, and the weeks into months, and Penelope found herself falling into a routine with Mrs. Dashwood. Side by side, the women worked well until Penelope was no longer capable and had to be confined to her bed at the behest of her daughter.

"I confess I am quite eager to be done with it," Penelope said on a warm summer day, while Mrs. Dashwood hovered over her. Eventually, Mrs. Dashwood, who had turned from a widowed employer to a maternal figure, threw the windows open and stuck her head out.

"It is a fine day outside," Mrs. Dashwood said over her shoulders. "You ought to go out and stretch your legs."

Penelope glanced down at the covers and pulled them up to her chest. "I do not believe it is a good idea."

Mrs. Dashwood placed both hands on her hips. "Nonsense. It is a fine idea. I will not be able to accompany you, but I feel certain you will be fine."

Penelope sighed. "You have been most kind to me, Mrs. Dashwood, but I do not think you understand that other people do not share your…sentiments."

Mrs. Dashwood frowned. "You must keep your chin up, my dear. There are plenty of people who will talk, and they will say many unkind things, but you must rise above it."

Penelope glanced up. "What if they are true?"

"There is nothing to be done about that."

Except that Penelope did blame herself.

Her father had warned her about men like Simon. Those who believed themselves to be above the law and above reproach, who committed sins freely without any consideration for those they hurt, or their mortal souls. In spite of her better judgement, Penelope had ignored her father's words and had even gone so far as to justify her behaviour with Simon. During their courtship, he had made her feel seen and cherished and better than she had in a long time. Although her poor father had done his best, being forced to raise a little girl alone had taken its toll on him.

And she did not blame him for not being able to give her the guidance and care she needed. The kind her dearly departed mother would've imparted. Unfortunately, Penelope's mother had died when she was scarcely four, and her father had moved from one vicarage to the next in search of gainful employment.

You are a fool, Penelope. You should've kept your wits about you, girl.

There was nothing more to be done.

But she would not subject herself to the pointing and whispering of the villagers. While they tolerated her presence for Mrs. Dashwood's sake, none of them had made a secret of their loathing and contempt for her. Even the doctor who tended to her seemed reluctant, and it was only because of Mrs. Dashwood's insistence and her firm nature that he had relented and taken Penelope into his care.

Thank heavens for that.

Still, the rest of the village was not likely to be swayed to her cause, not by Mrs. Dashwood or otherwise. As far as they were concerned, an unmarried and pregnant woman was only deserving of their ire and their judgement. Only Mrs. Dashwood saw fit to treat her with kindness and respect, so she kept to the cottage whenever she could, and only ventured into the village when it was necessary.

Mrs. Dashwood loomed over and gave her a small smile. "Whatever has befallen you, I am sure you did not mean for matters to take such a turn."

Penelope cleared her throat. "I did not."

Mrs. Dashwood held her head high. "In time, it will pass, and people will forget the circumstances that brought you here."

Penelope searched her face. "What of my baby? I do not wish for them to be treated poorly because of my mistake."

"My dear, your lapse in judgement will not define you for the rest of your life," Mrs. Dashwood said with a lift of her chin. "And it will not define your child either."

Penelope's chest tightened. "Do you really believe so?"

Mrs. Dashwood reached for her hands and patted them. "We shall make certain of it."

Penelope did not have the heart to tell Mrs. Dashwood the truth.

In spite of the washerwoman's kindness and the comfort and care she had so graciously lavished upon her, Penelope knew she could not stay for much longer. Once she was sufficiently recovered, and her baby well enough to travel, she intended to make her way to the city.

There, she wanted to search for gainful employment in order to better provide for herself and her daughter. In the city, she would reinvent herself as a widow, having lost her husband some years back to some unnamed illness. Given the bountiful opportunities present, she did not doubt that no one would think to look too long at her or her daughter.

But she loathed to leave the home of Mrs. Dashwood.

Some days later, in the dead of night when the doctor was summoned, it was Mrs. Dashwood who had remained by her side while she pushed and panted. Her entire body hurt and was covered in sweat while Doctor Rollins examined her. He said nothing as Mrs. Dashwood brought in scissors, towels, and a bowl filled with water. For hours, Penelope tossed and turned, wave after wave of pain building within her, with Mrs. Dashwood's voice floating in and out of focus.

In the early hours of the morning, she welcomed a little girl who cried and wailed until she was placed in her mother's arm. Exhausted and spent, Penelope barely had time to regard her daughter, her heart bursting with joy before she was taken away to be cleaned. Doctor Rollins did a quick examination of her before stiffly offering his congratulations. He took his leave shortly after, leaving her in the capable hands of Mrs. Dashwood, who insisted that she'd welcomed many babies into the world. When she was done cleaning the baby, she placed her back into Penelope's arms and left the two of them alone.

Years later, when Penelope made her way to the city, with her daughter in tow, she fell on hard times. Not only did she fail to find any meaningful employment, but she had also contracted an illness that settled into her bones and left her feeling weak and tired. For months, she scoured the city, doing everything within her power to secure employment, only to fail miserably. Months after her arrival, she found herself on the streets, on a brusque winter night, alone and desolate.

The streets around her were empty, save for the occasional gentleman who stumbled past, deep in the throes of drink. Penelope ducked into the alley, hiding her daughter behind her. She brought her back to rest against the cold brick wall and waited to regain her strength. When her vision grew blurry and her chest tightened, she wrapped her daughter in a bundle and reached for her hand.

"I am sorry, my darling," Penelope whispered, each breath laboured and difficult. "I have failed you."

And now her poor daughter was all alone in the world.

It was not enough that she did not have a father.

She was to be left without a mother, too.

For the rest of the night, Penelope struggled, fighting off the eternal sleep that beckoned her. When she grew too weak, she tugged on her daughter's hand and sang to her. She could not make sense of the lyrics, or whether or not her daughter understood what was happening. All she knew was that she would not make it till morning. The world around her turned from pitch black to dark grey, and Penelope's breath hitched in her throat.

She tilted her head back and looked up at the sky.

Hues of red and orange lit up the early morning sky. There wasn't a cloud in sight as she studied the heavens, a strange sense of peace washing over her. By the time the sun climbed up, Penelope knew she was drawing her last breath. She took one last look at her daughter, released a deep shuddering breath, and a single tear slid down her cheeks.

Lord almighty, watch over my daughter. Keep her safe and under your care, always. Amen.

With that, her hand went limp, and her departed body grew absolutely still.

***

Travel worn and in a foul mood, Simon Bloom came to a stop in front of the Devon's estate. He stood on the other side of a small gate and frowned. With a slight shake of his head, he adjusted the lapels of his jacket and lowered his head. Then he made his way to the back door, where Penelope had stood many months before, beaming and smiling at him.

He did not know why she had stopped writing to him.

Or why he had not heard from her in nearly a year.

It had been eleven months since he had last set eyes on her.

Between the affairs of the estate, and his mother's mysterious illness, he had not been able to take leave. Coupled with the fact that his letters had gone unanswered, Simon had assumed the worst. Now he was finally ready to confront Penelope and have the answers he needed. Having spent months nursing his broken heart and wondering what had become of her, he was tired of not knowing.

Here was his chance to learn the truth of the matter, regardless of how badly it hurt.

So, he brought his hand up to the back door and knocked. The door opened to reveal Mrs. Knightley, the elderly housekeeper dressed in a dark dress, with her hair pulled back and in an unkind smile.

"Good morning. I am sorry to disturb you, but I am here to see Ms. Wickham."

Mrs. Knightley frowned. "Ms. Wickham is no longer employed here."

Simon blinked. "I beg your pardon?"

Mrs. Knightly drew herself up to her full height and peered at him. "Young man, you ought to do yourself a favour and forget all about Ms. Wickham."

"Excuse me?"

"She was asked to leave when it was discovered she was with child," Mrs. Knightly revealed after a quick glance over her shoulders. "Imagine the scandal she would've brought upon this house. An unmarried woman carrying a child out of wedlock. The shame of it all."

With a heavy heart, Simon had taken his leave of the housekeeper. For months after, he wandered, searching high and low for Penelope, and hoping against hope that he would find her. His journey had taken him all over the country, stopping at every tavern and village along the way. Unfortunately, the more he looked, the more dejected he felt until a year later, he was forced to give up his search by his mother and return to the affairs of his estate.

Seeing his melancholy state, his mother insisted that he cast off whatever ailed him and turn his gaze to the future. So, he threw himself into his work and focused on expanding the estate and pouring all of his time and energy into his personal affairs. In time, he hoped that the memory of Penelope would not haunt him as vividly.

Had the child been his?

Simon had no way of knowing for sure, and he did not wish to torment himself with the memory of a woman who had vanished. Two years later, Simon found himself enjoying the smiles and company of Cecelia Shepard, daughter of an old friend of his mother's. When the two of them had spent enough time together, knowing what was expected of him, he had asked Cecelia to marry him.

Yet, on the day of their wedding, it was Penelope he saw, and he found himself praying that good fortune had found her. As he took his vows on that quiet spring day, in the presence of family and friends, he vowed to keep Penelope tucked away in his heart, safe and sound. And he prayed life had been kinder to her, allowing her a reprieve and a life befitting of her kind and loving nature.

Chapter Five

"Sir?"

Simon blinked and twisted his head, coming face to face with his coachman, whose eyebrows were drawn together, bright eyes filled with confusion. "What is it?"

The coachman straightened his back. "Will you be needing me to take you anywhere else, sir?"

Simon gave a slight shake of his head and ran a hand over his face. He had no idea how long he stood there, reliving his memories, but the longer he did, the stronger the pull felt. Half of him was tempted to climb back up the stairs, pound on the door, and beg for forgiveness. Given everything Penelope had endured because of his folly, it was the least he could do.

Would his daughter ever forgive him?

He stiffened and turned away from the window.

For a while, he turned the matter over and over in his head, wondering how Lilly had come to be in the household of a seamstress and her husband. He lamented the fact that he had not thought to ask Shelly, who had doubtless learned everything there was to know about Lilly during their tête-à-tête.

Yet, he did not wish to drag Shelly further into his affairs.

Not when the knowledge of Lilly's true identity was likely to hurt her.

And Cecelia.

In truth, he did love his family dearly, and with his entire heart, but he had never stopped thinking of Penelope or wishing for her. Now, learning of the fate of his daughter all these years later was like coming up for air after being underwater for too long. Everything felt sharper and far clearer than it had in a long time. His only remaining question was what had become of his beloved Penelope.

Had she taken refuge with the Chalmers, too?

For the life of him, Simon did not know, but he supposed it did not matter much. Slowly, he turned back to the window, where Lilly still stood with her arms folded over her chest, and a thoughtful expression on her face. As soon as she twisted her head to the side, the hint of a smile playing on the edge of her lips, something in his stomach unfurled and blossomed. A lump rose in the back of his throat and tears burned the back of his eyes.

Forgive me, Penelope. I should have looked harder.

During his brief glimpse of her, Simon had ascertained that she was in good health and well-fed. He was immensely grateful to the Chalmers for that, who had, quite clearly, bestowed upon her a great deal of love, care, and affection. While they did not have much in the way of money and property, he was nevertheless glad that they had given Penelope the best life they could. Given their circumstances, he knew it was not something he could ever repay them for.

But he would not stop trying.

Lilly had done well for herself.

She did, after all, live in a clean and modest room with her family and was employed as a seamstress. According to his daughter, she was among the best in the city, known for her quick, nimble fingers and her bright disposition. Simon was suddenly filled with the urge to take Lilly away to the country house where he could spend hours in her company, learning everything there was to know about the young lady.

Alas, he knew it would not be possible.

Not only would the gesture arouse suspicion, but if the truth of her circumstances were to come to light, it was Lilly who would be forced to pay the price. Considering everything she had endured to get to where she was, Simon had no desire to inflict further pain upon her, not even for his own selfish needs. Doubtless, she had suffered much, being forced to grow up without knowing her father and with Penelope struggling to provide for both of them.

Simon did not think the world had been kind to either of them.

Still, he prayed that a small modicum of compassion had been dealt to them. Nevertheless, Simon found himself grateful that it had all worked out in the end. Had he found his daughter under lesser circumstances, he was not sure what he would've done.

People began to rush past in either direction, with a few of them pausing to stare at him, the well-dressed gentleman in a poorer area of the city, staring at a window. He felt their eyes on him, but he could not bring himself to care, not when he wanted to gaze upon his long-lost daughter for as long as humanly possible. Eventually, Lilly moved away from the window and turned her back on him. Simon stared at her back, and something in his stomach tightened.

Simon turned the matter over and over in his head, eventually deciding against it. With a deep sigh, he forced his gaze away from the house and felt the warmth of the sun on the back of his neck. He took one step, then another, and ducked into the awaiting carriage. As soon as the coachman was settled, Simon stuck his head out the window and gave him instructions. Then he leaned back against the seats and buried his head in his hands.

Lilly would not want anything to do with him if she knew the truth.

Knowing that all those years ago he had given up on Penelope, assuming she did not want to be found did not sit well with him especially not that he had stumbled upon their daughter. Having spent an entire year searching high and low for her, he had not been left with much choice, particularly considering there was an estate that needed his attention. With an entire household staff and tenants depending upon him for their livelihood, Simon had not thought it wise to ignore them any longer. While he would've liked nothing more than to spend the rest of his life reminiscing and living off of the memory of

Penelope, it was his mother who had pushed him into moving on.

And she had been right to do so.

No good would've come of clinging to a ghost.

As the carriage lurched forward and the sound of hooves reverberated inside of his head, his thoughts turned to Lilly once more. He tried but failed to imagine all she had endured in order to turn into the resilient and kind young lady she was today. Thankfully, she had been surrounded by honest and hard-working folk. Again, Simon doubted his decision to delay an introduction, all the way until he pulled up outside of a building situated in the middle of the city in a nicer neighbourhood with brick houses and foliage that was well tended to.

Simon stepped out of the carriage and tilted his head back.

After a brief hesitation, he walked through the front doors and paused. Several people glanced up, and Simon was immediately ushered into a room. A tray with tea and biscuits was brought in as soon as he sat down. He took off his hat and placed it in his lap. At his sides, his hands clenched and unclenched until his lawyer came in, looking harried with a thin sheen of sweat on his forehead.

"Mr. Bloom." Richard took a seat opposite him and took out a handkerchief, pausing to dab his face. "I was not told that you would be coming today. I apologize for the delay."

"I did not send word," Simon told him after a brief pause. "I understand this is short notice, but a matter of utmost importance has just come to my attention."

Richard sat up straighter and peered at him. "Is everything alright, sir? Shall I call for a doctor?"

"Nonsense." Simon waved his comment away and leaned back against the chair. "I am quite well. I assure you."

Richard frowned. "Forgive me, sir, but you do look quite pale."

Simon cleared his throat. "Think nothing of it. Now, onto the matter at hand."

Richard sat up straighter and fixed his gaze on him. "What can I help you with, Mr. Bloom?"

"I wish to have papers drawn up immediately. Do not ask me questions regarding the person in question."

***

"But you did not invite him in?"

"Papa wanted to, but he looked to be in a great hurry."

Polly glanced up and swatted at an errant lock of hair. "Was he well-dressed?"

Lilly kept her gaze fixed on the fine material between her fingers. "Mr. Bloom is a well-dressed gentleman, yes, but he seemed to be quite upset."

Polly's eyebrows drew together. "Do you think it has anything to do with Mrs. Bloom? Surely they cannot expect us to be done with her dress so soon."

Lilly shrugged. "I cannot say for certain, but I do believe his feelings were of a more personal nature."

And she wondered if it had anything to do with his daughter.

Had Shelly confided in her father regarding the resemblance?

Lilly turned the matter over and over in her head, but the more she thought about it, the less sense it made. Not only did Shelly have far better things to do than to dwell on the uncanny resemblance between her and a seamstress, but Lilly also doubted her father, a well-to-do gentleman, would have given the matter much thought. While Mr. Bloom might have indulged his daughter, allowing her a brief flight of fancy, it was unlikely he encouraged it to go further.

Not when there were serious ramifications to consider.

For the life of her, Lilly could not understand any of it. Yet, she had felt a strange tingling in her stomach upon setting her sight on Mr. Bloom's kind, bright eyes and his thick head of hair. There was something altogether pleasing and inviting about him. So much so that she had begun to wonder if she had taken leave of her senses altogether.

Why did she find herself drawn to the gentleman in question?

He reminded her a great deal of her own father, being of a similar build and quiet nature, but there was nothing else the two of them had in common. However, there was something altogether paternal and comforting about Simon, even if she had only spent a few minutes in his presence. While she did not know the gentleman well enough to be making such assumptions, she knew she felt welcome and appreciated in his presence.

And what a strange feeling it was!

With a shake of her head, Lilly endeavoured to push the thought out of her mind entirely. Not only was she unlikely to see Mister Bloom again anytime soon, but she was also sure he had not given her a second thought after their unusual meeting a few days prior. She rubbed a hand over her face, offered Polly a tired smile, and rolled her shoulders.

"I will go and check on Mama."

Polly didn't look up when she replied. "Would you like me to help? Is there anything I can do?"

"We have been at this for quite some time, Pol," Lilly pointed out. "I think you had better stop and stretch your legs."

Polly glanced up and blinked. Then she turned her attention to the window and the afternoon sun in the centre of the sky, peeking out from behind gathering clouds. Wordlessly, she stood up and let out a deep and shuddering sigh. Afterwards, she gave Lilly a grateful smile before crossing over to the door. Through the walls, Lilly heard her call out for her grandmother, followed by Mrs. Wodehouse's response, before everything went quiet. Walking quietly, Lilly made her way into the room and came to a stop in front of her mother's sleeping form.

Her breathing was even and steady, and Rosie's eyes were fixed on the ceiling.

Lilly knelt down onto the floor and adjusted the folds of her dress around her. "Is there anything I can get you?"

Rosie blinked and twisted to face Lilly, a shadow moving over her face. "Nothing at all, my dear. You already do far too much for me."

Lilly shook her head and reached for her mother's hands. "I do not do enough."

Rosie frowned. "Nonsense. I am quite fortunate to have you, my darling Lilly. I do not know what would have become of me if it were not for you."

Bright sunlight poured in through the windows, giving the room a soft, buttery glow. Lilly's eyes swept over the room before they settled on her mother, taking in the tired lines on her face, and the emotions lingering in her eyes.

"I do not know what would have become of me," Lilly said in a clear voice. "You took me in when I had nowhere else to go. I cannot thank you enough."

Rosie withdrew her hands and brought her forehead to a rest against Lilly's. "I knew from the moment I set eyes on you that you needed me, and you will always be my daughter, Lilly, blood or not."

Lilly's eyes filled with tears. "I know."

Rosie withdrew and studied her daughter's face. "There is something troubling you."

Lilly cleared her throat and brought her head to a rest in her mother's lap. "I know that speaking of the past pains you. I do not mean to be ungrateful, but I cannot help but wonder about my father."

Rosie stilled. "Your father?"

"Speaking of my mother is too painful for you. I am sure you must have loved her, but I have never heard you speak of my father."

Rosie stroked Lilly's hair. "I did not know your father."

Lilly glanced up and swallowed. "You did not meet him?"

Rosie shook her head. "I did not. I am sorry, my love. I know you have many questions, but I do not have the answers you seek."

Lilly sat back on her legs and stared at her mother. "I wish you did."

Rose's expression turned sad. "So do I."

Lilly opened her mouth, then shook her head. "I had better be getting back to the sewing."

Rosie reached for Lilly's hands and squeezed. "Your father and I love you very much. I pray you always know that."

Lilly's throat turned dry. "I love you, too."

With that, she rose to her feet and gave her mother's hands a tight squeeze. When Rosie released her hands a few moments later, Lilly turned and took her leave. She returned with a glass of water, but her mother had flipped onto her side and was fast asleep. Quietly, Lilly set the glass down and drew in a sharp breath. As soon as she stepped out of the room, she released it and brought her head to a rest against the wall.

What did you hope to accomplish with your questions, Lilly? You are being cruel and unkind to the people who raised you. Rosie and Peter are the only parents you have ever known, and they are all you need in this world.

Considering how fortunate she was, she did not understand why she could not forget the matter altogether. On the streets of the city, there were far too many orphans, and too many children with only their mothers for company. Lilly herself saw them often; the haunted looks in their eyes and the sadness on their faces stayed with her.

Why, she herself had come too close to being amongst their ranks.

Were it not for Rosie and Peter, a vile and wretched fate would have awaited her.

"Are you alright?"

Lilly pushed herself off the wall and came face to face with Polly, who lingered in the doorway in her faded old brown dress. "Yes. Do not trouble yourself on my account. How is your grandmother?"

"She is resting," Polly replied, pausing to push her hair out of her face. "Someday, I should quite like to take her to the country."

"I think Mama and Papa would enjoy a trip to the country as well." Lilly offered her friend a smile on the way past. "We would all enjoy it a great deal, I think."

Polly smiled. "I reckon we could take a trip soon. Our wages ought to be enough."

Together, the two of them sat back down near the fire in chairs that were facing each other and a wooden table in between them. Lilly picked up the dress and began to hum under her breath. Across from her, Polly did the same, a brusque breeze, carrying the scent of earth and grass wafting in through the open window. Now and again, Lilly heard the clatter of hooves and conversations rise and fall before everything went quiet.

As soon as their voices drifted off and they lapsed into silence, someone rapped on the door. Lilly's eyebrows drew together as she stood up and set the dress down. "Are we expecting anyone today?"

Polly shook her head and rose to her feet. "No, we are not."

Lilly walked over to the door and through the slit, she peeked, finding herself staring at a short man with dark hair brushed back over his head. He wore a double-breasted coat, a striped waistcoat, trousers and a small back tie. With a frown, she twisted the knob, and he stood up straighter, holding a sealed envelope in his hands.

"Miss Lilly Chalmer?"

Lilly stood up straighter. "Yes."

He held out the envelope and waited for her to take it. "Have a good day, ma'am."

Lilly glanced down at the envelope, then back up at his face. "I'm afraid you must be mistaken."

The man shook his head. "There are instructions in the envelope, Miss. Please excuse me."

With that, he bowed his head and took a few steps back. Then he spun on his heels and hurried back down the stairs. Lilly watched him until he left. Still, she stood there, unable to bring herself to close the door. Wordlessly, Polly ushered her back inside and let the door click shut. As soon as it did, Lilly snapped to attention and turned the envelope over. Her name was written on the back in bold and cursive handwriting.

Her fingers trembled as she ripped it open.

When she scanned the contents of the letter, another piece of paper fluttered to the ground. Hastily, Lilly bent down to pick it up. Over and over, she read the contents, scarcely believing her own eyes. She collapsed into her chair, pressed the letter to her chest, and stared at Polly.

"What is the matter?" Polly peered at her, her eyes darting over to the letter. "What's happened?"

"I have been left a sum of money," Lilly told her in a strange voice. "I am to be given an allowance henceforth until the end of my days."

Polly's mouth fell open. "What do you mean?"

Lilly sat up straighter and ran a hand over her face. She could barely hear anything past the pounding of her heart that prompted bile to rise in the back of her throat. "A bank account has been opened in my name, and there is already a vast sum of money there."

Polly's mouth snapped shut. "Oh, Lilly. How wonderful this must be for you! Wherever did the money come from?"

Lilly held the letter up to her face and read it again. "It does not say. Only that it comes from a benefactor who wishes to remain unknown."

Polly pulled Lilly up to her feet and hugged her. "This calls for a celebration. We must tell your parents at once."

Lilly stared down at the envelope, her eyes lingering on the distinguished seal on the back, but she could no more make out what it was than she could make sense of the events that had transpired within the last hour. Wordlessly, she lowered herself back onto the chair and buried her head in her hands. Still, the thudding in her heart continued, but little by little, the tightness in her chest subsided. When she felt a hand on her back rubbing her shoulders, she lowered her hands and looked up at Polly.

"I am sure this must be overwhelming," Polly began with a small smile. "But surely it is a blessing."

Lilly swallowed. "I cannot say for certain."

Although she was grateful beyond belief for the generosity of her secret benefactor, particularly considering the generous amount already deposited into the account, she could not bring herself to rejoice. Not when the anonymous benefactor herself plagued her.

Briefly, she thought of Mister Bloom before pushing the thought away.

It could not have been him, not when they did not mean anything to each other. For the life of her, Lilly could not understand where the money had come from, and the more she thought about it, the less the entire affair made sense. After some time, Lilly stood up, and after a long conversation with Polly, her friend took her dress and withdrew. Upon her father's return, she beckoned him into her mother's room, and the three of them sat down together. When she was done with her miraculous revelation, her parents sat back, wearing equally stunned and pale expressions.

"And you are sure the letter did not have any stipulations?"

Lilly held the letter out to her father and shook her head. "None whatsoever. The amount is to be given to me every few months to do with as I please."

Peter scanned the letter and turned it over. "It looks to be written on a fine piece of paper."

"It is a generous amount indeed," Rosie murmured faintly. "Far more than both of us can make in an entire lifetime."

Even if they were to work hard for the rest of their days, the Chalmers were unlikely to ever see such an amount. Overwhelmed with joy and gratitude, Lilly drew her parents closer to her, and the three of them wept and laughed together. Emotion bubbled up within her, and by the time she drew away, she turned to her father, who spun her around the room while her mother applauded their little impromptu dance.

At that moment, the Chalmers could not have been more grateful to have each other.

Chapter Six

"Have you had any luck discovering the identity of your benefactor?"

Lilly glanced up from her work and blinked, her friend's features sharpening into focus. "No, I have not."

Polly smiled. "Perhaps you have a secret admirer."

Lilly frowned. "I do not think that anyone would go to such lengths for my sake."

And without revealing their identity, no less.

Would it not make more sense for the gentleman in question to step forward so she could thank him properly? The more she turned the matter over in her head, the less sense it made. Over the past week, she had done everything within her power to discover the secret nature of her wealthy benefactor, to no avail.

Lilly had met with the lawyers and several employees at the bank, only to be met with the same resistance. All of them had been given similar instructions to keep his identity a secret. All she knew for certain was that it was someone who was in possession of a fortune and had decided to bestow some of it upon her.

Having spent the entirety of her life working as a seamstress and keeping to herself, she did not believe herself to be special. Nor was she a great beauty in possession of any great skills. On the contrary, beyond her lucrative work as a seamstress, Lilly had very little else to boast of, including an education that had been for naught, considering she had not been able to put it to good use. Much to her dismay, Lilly was unlikely to be given any kind of employment pertaining to her sharp mind. Instead, she would likely spend her days tending to clothes like her family. There was a quiet nobility to be found in her type of employment, and she took great pride in being able to provide for herself and her family.

Especially given that her father was no longer able to work.

As of a week ago, he was waylaid from the gentleman's club with the establishment, having spent the better part of the last two years trying to push him out the door. Although Peter had served them well and with honour for the better part of thirty years, the fact remained that he was no longer a young and healthy man capable of undertaking the more straining tasks within the establishment. Her father had, naturally, taken the entire thing in stride, smiling and nodding along as if he hadn't a care in the world.

Only his family knew the truth.

And Lilly, in particular, had engaged in many conversations with him regarding his future and how helpless he felt having been forced to seek work elsewhere. Since their last conversation, Lilly had carried around guilt and apprehension, and for the first time since receiving news of her fortune, she knew why.

Neither Rosie nor Peter ought to work one more day in their life.

Not while Lilly was alive.

Given all of the love and kindness they had shown her over the years, particularly when she was not of their flesh and blood, it was the least she could do. Some hours later, having finished with Mrs. Bloom's dress, Polly returned to her grandmother. Lilly, on the other hand, stood by the window, watching the streets of the city below. Few people were out now that the moon was high in the sky, and there was a smattering of stars sprinkled throughout.

Still, she gazed upon the streets as if they held all the answers.

Now and again, she heard voices rise, followed by a group of men that sounded deep in their cups, bellowing at the top of their lungs. She leaned against the wall and smiled at them, wondering what cares they had in their lives. A few times she even spotted a few scantily clad women tucked against the men's sides, their smiles crimson, and their skin glistening with sweat.

A while later, Lilly forced herself away from the window and reached for the oil lamp next to the fireplace. She held it up to her face and crept forward, the floor creaking beneath her feet. At the end of the hallway, she stopped and brought her hand up to the door. When she heard a soft voice reply, she pushed the door open and the light cast shadows across the walls.

Her father sat in a chair across from the bed, his hands folded in his lap. Rosie was propped against the pillow, a smile stretched across her face. Both of them turned to face her with bright smiles and loving gazes. Lilly's heart jumped into her throat as she stepped further into the room and let the door click shut behind her. Once it did, she took a few steps forward and released a deep breath.

"I have a matter of great importance I wish to discuss."

Rosie's smile vanished. "Is everything alright? Are you well?"

Lilly nodded. "I am well."

Peter sat up straighter, and his eyebrows drew together. "Is it Polly? She did not bid us good night, and she normally does. I hope the two of you have not gotten into an argument."

Lilly shook her head. "There is nothing amiss with Polly. She hurried home because of Mrs. Wodehouse."

"She is a good granddaughter," Rosie murmured, a sad expression on her face. "I cannot understand why her father has all but abandoned her."

"He did not abandon her, Mama."

"He might as well have," Peter argued with a shake of his head. "He has not seen her in years, and he only inquires after her in passing as if she were not his. That is not a real father, my dear."

Lilly swallowed. "Not everyone is as fortunate as I am. I am blessed to have you both."

"And we are blessed to have you," Rose finished with a smile.

Lilly was reminded of her good fortune every time she felt Polly's gaze linger on them, or she saw the pain hidden in her eyes when Lilly and her parents gathered around the table and laughed. While she knew her friend did not begrudge her a good family, nor would Polly want it to be taken away, however, Lilly couldn't ignore how difficult it was for Polly. Being forced to witness a happy family day in and day out, while her own grandmother wilted away. Each day, Lilly breathed a sigh of relief when news of Mrs. Wodehouse's demise did not reach her ears.

As it was, she knew it was only a matter of time before it did.

It filled her with a sense of unease and dread.

Lilly loved Polly dearly, and the two of them had grown up side by side, becoming inseparable over the years. While there was little she would not do for her oldest and dearest friend, Lilly knew that cheating death was beyond her capabilities. Even her newfound wealth would not delay the inevitable, as much as she wished it would. In truth, all she could do for Polly was be there and pray that when the day did come, she would be standing right by Polly's side to support and help her in whatever way she can.

In the meantime, all she could do was pray for dear old Mrs. Wodehouse.

Lord, I ask that you watch over her, and keep her in your good graces. She is in need of your guidance and your assistance. Now and always. Amen.

Peter beckoned Lilly forward, the furrow between his brows deepening. "You seem troubled, my dear. Is everything alright?"

Lilly blinked and was brought back to the present with a jolt. "I have been thinking about my recent change of circumstance."

Peter sat up straighter and adopted a serious expression. "I see. And what have you decided?"

"I wish to move somewhere else," Lilly replied after a brief pause. "I realize that is a big undertaking, but I have heard of the areas being established on the outskirts of London, and I feel certain we can be quite happy there."

"Why would we move?" Rosie pulled the covers up to her chins and shivered. "We are quite content here."

"You need to get better, Mama," Lilly told her, before she walked over and knelt down by the foot of the bed. "The doctor said that you are in desperate need of warmth."

Rosie waved her comment away. "I shall be quite fine, I assure you."

Lilly clasped her hands together and cleared her throat. "Let me help you, Mama. As you and Papa have done for me over the years. It is the least I can do. I have no use for all of that money, anyway."

"You could invest it," Peter suggested. "I am certain a great many things could be done, but you should not waste your money."

Lilly twisted to face him. "Do you think it a waste to ensure that the two of you are well taken care of? And that three of us live in a more comfortable house?"

Peter coughed and ran a hand over her face. "We are quite comfortable here, my dear. There is no need for such extravagances, I assure you."

Lilly pushed herself off the bed and walked over to her father. She wrapped both of her arms around him and squeezed. "Papa, you and Mama have done a great deal and sacrificed so much. Please allow me to do this for you. I can buy us a cottage."

With plenty of room, sunlight, and none of them having to work hard to earn a living again, she was sure it was to be a good start for all of them. Lilly had already inquired into the matter, courtesy of the bank, and they had presented her with several options befitting her new status. One of them was a cottage on the outskirts of London with three bedrooms overlooking a garden.

She imagined Rosie bathed in sunlight, regaining her strength, and it filled her with a renewed sense of purpose. Over the next hour, she debated the merits of such an endeavour until the Chalmers were forced to, quite reluctantly, concede to her point. In the morning, she was to go to the bank and see about the necessary paperwork. Lilly was beside herself with excitement.

But first, there was the matter of deciding precisely which cottage would do.

That night, Lilly tossed and turned on her mattress by the fireplace until the first patches of morning light lit up the sky. As the world turned from a bleak grey to hues of orange and red, she stood up and stretched her arms over her head. Quietly, Lilly opened the door to their room and called out for Polly. Her friend stepped into the doorway in her nightgown and a glazed look on her face.

"What is it?"

"How would you like to live in a cottage?"

Polly blinked. "I beg your pardon?"

"I am going to look at cottages with Mama and Papa today, and I should very much like your opinion, as you are to be moving in with us."

Polly opened and closed her mouth several times. "I do not understand."

"You did not think I would leave you behind, did you?" Lilly covered the distance between them and drew Polly into her arms. Her friend shuddered and broke into tears. Polly's entire body shook as she clung to Lilly and muttered. "You are my sister, Polly, and I will not leave you or Mrs. Wodehouse behind. You are, after all, family."

Polly sniffed and drew back. "It is a terrible imposition. We could not possibly—"

"You *can* possibly," Lilly interrupted with a smile. "And you will. I will not hear of anything else."

Polly gave her a grateful smile. "I do not know how I can ever thank you."

"Your friendship is thanks enough," Lilly told her, pausing to take both of Polly's hands in hers. "You have been like a sister to me for years, and for that, I am eternally grateful."

Polly squeezed her hands and said nothing.

Wordlessly, Lilly drew away and back into the room. She found her parents dressed and beaming at her, hopeful expressions on their faces. After she changed, they helped themselves to a quick breakfast of porridge and tea. Then they ventured onto the streets of London.

It was an uncommonly warm day with the sun set against a backdrop of clear blue skies. Now and again, Lilly paused and tilted her head back, enjoying the warmth of the sun on the bridge of her nose. Out of the corner of her eye, she saw the Chalmers do the same, with Rosie in particular regaining some of the colour in her cheeks. It seemed to Lilly as if her mother was much improved already, and she could not wait to see the difference once they moved into a cottage.

Rosie would blossom and thrive there once more.

By the time they made it to the newly established area on the outskirts of London, the whole of the city was bustling and teeming with life. Lilly weaved in and out of people, smiling at street vendors and laughing at the children who shrieked and ran past her. Rosie and Peter remained subdued until they reached a row of stone cottages with small gardens out front. In silence, the three of them examined one after the other, growing more and more impressed with each passing second.

Her parents, in particular, could not stop murmuring about their good fortune, and how blessed they were to have Lilly in their lives. She saw the tears in their eyes and the awe written on their faces, and it left a pleasant warmth in the pit of her stomach. When it came time to decide, Lilly insisted that such a decision could not be made lightly.

So, she took them to a bakery in one of the more affluent neighbourhoods of the city, where people wore their Sunday finest, and all of the buildings were well tended to. There, they took a seat at a table next to the window and indulged in fine pastries and hot tea. Lilly munched slowly, savouring each piece as if it were her last, and delighting in the array of flavours dancing on the tip of her tongue.

What a delightful day it was turning into.

As soon as they were done eating, they made their way back to their own building, beaming and flushed with pleasure. In the midst of their discussion, Lilly revealed her intention to move Polly and her grandmother into the cottage with them, and as she had expected, the Chalmers were thrilled.

Peter took her hands in his and squeezed. "Of course they are welcome to come and live with us. I can think of nothing else."

"And we shall be glad of the company," Rosie added, before lowering herself onto the chair in front of the fire. Peter dropped Lilly's hands and went over to his wife. He bent down in front of the fireplace and stoked it to life, the smell of ash and burning wood filling the place. Then he took a few steps back and folded his arms over his chest.

"I still have my concerns," Peter told her, his eyes focused on the flames. "I wonder if such an expense is necessary."

"We have, after all, been blessed with this room," Rosie added in a quiet voice. "We do not wish you for to mismanage your fortune, my love."

"I have already spoken to the bank regarding my investment," Lilly assured them, pausing to tuck her hair behind her ears. She ran her hands along the front of her cream-colored dress. "Everybody is in agreement regarding my decision."

Peter scoffed. "It is a bank, my dear. As long as you spend money, they are quite happy."

Lilly laughed. "That is unkind, Papa, really. I am sure they only mean to help."

And given how much she wanted to help Rosie and cure her ailments, she could think of no better solution. In time, she hoped that her mother's arthritis would cease to exist altogether, but she knew it was only wishful thinking. At most, her mother's health would improve in time, and she would regain more movement in her joints, but anything more than that was a miracle.

Yet, Lilly found herself wishing for one.

A week ago, she had been toiling over dresses by the dying embers of a fire, while Polly sat across from her and hummed. While Lilly had been prone to flights of fancy, like any young girl on the cusp of womanhood, even her wildest dreams could not have led her there. Should she wish it, Lilly did not have to work one more day for the rest of her life, and she and the Chalmers would still be able to live a good and comfortable life.

What more could she possibly want?

As they usually did, her thoughts turned to her birth parents, and their role in all of this. Although Rosie assured her that her mother had been given a proper burial it was Lilly's father that Rosie refused to speak of. Or, she simply did not know who the man was given her strained relationship with her sister during the last years of her life. Given the current set of circumstances, Lilly had no desire to ruin the celebratory mood with her line of questioning and insistence on finding answers.

Perhaps she ought to hire an investigator.

Unfortunately, the more she thought about it, the less sense it made. Not only did she not have any names to go off, but since she had come to them half-starved and in bad shape, no one had been able to determine her exact age. Thus, it would be difficult to determine when exactly Lilly had been brought into the world, or when her birth parents had wed.

Oh, how maddening it all was not to learn the whole truth.

Later, when the Chalmers retired from the evening, looking to be in far better spirits and having laughed and dined well, Lilly sat down in the chair by the fireplace. She picked up the book she had begun to read and brought it up to her face. Only she could not bring herself to focus.

After some time had passed, and she found herself on the same page, she made a low frustrated noise and stood up. She came to stand by the window, and it was there that Rosie happened upon her daughter, staring at the streets below.

"Why do you look troubled, my dear?"

"I know that you do not wish me to speak of my mother," Lilly whispered, her voice catching towards the end. "I know she was a good woman, and you must have loved her, but there is so much I do not know."

Rosie wrapped her arms around Lilly's shoulders and hugged her. "I do not mean to upset you, my darling. There is much that I do not remember."

Lilly continued to stare at the empty and dark street below, scarcely able to make out anything in the soft light of the moon. Now and again, she made out the vague silhouette of men rushing past in either direction. Many of them wore fine clothes that were rumpled and had colour on their cheeks.

She turned away from and glanced over at her mother and her sunken cheeks. Time had not been kind to Rosie Chalmer, in spite of her generous spirit and her warm heart. Lilly wanted nothing more than to ensure that Rosie lived out the rest of her days in comfort and happiness.

"Can you not tell me anything about my father?"

Rosie released Lilly and exhaled. "I'm afraid I did not know your father."

Lilly frowned. "Can you not write to your family and inquire after him?"

Rosie cleared her throat. "No one else knew him either."

Lilly scrubbed a hand over her face. "How can that be? Surely, there must be someone who knows the truth about him."

Rosie lifted her gaze up to Lilly's face, and her expression turned pained. "Have we upset you in any way?"

Lilly's eyebrows drew together. "No, Mama. What makes you say that?"

Rosie sniffed and turned away, but not before Lilly saw the tear that rolled down her cheeks. "There are times when I wonder if we have not done enough. Perhaps there was more we could have done."

Lilly shook her head and drew her mother towards her. "Mama, that could not be further from the truth. You and Papa have given me a good life. You have shown me love and kindness when you did not have to, and for that I am immensely grateful."

Rosie's eyes filled with tears. "When you came to us, you were such a small and frail thing.

You were covered in dirt and sweat and looked as if you had not eaten in days. As soon as you saw me, you clung to me, and I knew then that you were my daughter. No matter if you did not come from me."

Lilly squeezed her mother's shoulders. "You are my mother, and Peter is my father. Nothing else matters."

And no matter her curiosity, it was not going to change what she knew in her heart to be true. The Chalmers were always meant to be her family. Shortly after their talk, Lilly ushered her mother into her room and closed the door behind her. She wandered into the sitting room and found herself glancing around the room at nothing in particular.

Someone rapped on the door.

Lilly crossed the room and peered through the slit, relieved to see Polly on the other side. She pulled her friend in, and the door clicked shut behind her. The floor creaked and groaned underneath their feet and long shadows were cast along the walls. Behind Polly, Lilly caught a brief glimpse of the crescent shaped moon before the two of them sat across from each other.

"My grandmother is beside herself with excitement," Polly told her, her entire face lighting up. "I truly cannot think of how to thank you."

Lilly shook her head. "I need no thanks."

"I will continue to work, of course," Polly said with a lift of her chin. "For I wish to continue to support myself and my grandmother and manage our own expenses."

"At least you will not have to worry about your living situation," Lilly offered with a small smile. "And as for expenses, we can discuss all of the details later. I do not want you to worry."

Polly leaned back in the chair and sighed.

Shadows danced and moved across her face, making her look far more vulnerable and youthful. Lilly's eyes moved over her, taking in her pale complexion, and the hair braided and draped her over her shoulders. Her eyes swept over the faded brown dress, and she frowned. Tomorrow, she was going to take Polly to a dressmaker in the city, and the two of them were going to make a few purchases.

Lilly was giddied with excitement.

Polly cleared her throat. "Have you had any luck discovering the identity of your benefactor?"

Lilly shook her head. "No, the bank was kind enough to put me in touch with the lawyers in charge of the case, but they were not helpful in that matter."

"They are still refusing to tell you his identity?"

Lilly nodded. "A young lawyer took pity on me, but the most he could tell me was that they had received instructions from another set of lawyers from another firm. Between the two firms, my affairs are being handled with the utmost discretion."

And secrecy.

Truthfully, it did not sit well with Lilly. She wanted nothing more than to gaze upon the person responsible for such a change in circumstances and express her gratitude. Considering everything he had done for them, it was the least she could do. Unfortunately, she was no closer to having the answers now than she was when she first had been told the news.

An entire week of inquires and beseeching had amounted to nothing.

Still, Lilly imagined it could be far worse.

"Perhaps he will come forward," Polly offered after a lengthy dance. The fire danced and crackled next to them, and outside an animal howled. "There is no reason for him not to."

"Unless he does not want the information to be made public," Lilly mused, leaning backwards into her chair and folded her hands in her lap. "I suppose I must respect his wishes either way."

"What makes you so certain it is a he?"

Lilly shrugged and pursed her lips together. "I cannot say for certain, only that it is a feeling I have."

Polly ran a hand over her face. "It is a most unusual feeling, is it not?"

Lilly released a deep breath. "It is."

"Do you believe it is a distant relation?"

Lilly paused and sat up straighter. "Sometimes, I wonder if it is my father."

Polly blinked. "Your father? Was he not poor?"

"I do not know. No one does. My mother does not know much regarding the matter, and if she does, she will not discuss it. The pain of her sister's loss still weighs heavily on her, and I do not wish to upset her."

Polly tilted her head to the side and studied Lilly's face. "But you still wish for answers."

"Would you not if you were in my place?"

Polly leaned forward and coughed. "I cannot say for certain. I have never known my mother, and as you know, my father did not wish to be saddled with my responsibility. Grandmother is the only family I have."

Lilly's hand darted out and closed around Polly's. "We are your family, too, Polly. No matter what happens. Rich or poor. You are as much a Chalmer as you are a Wodehouse."

Polly smiled tearfully. "Truly, I have been fortunate to have you as a friend, Lil. You are the reason I have gotten through many hard times."

"And you are my sister. Without you by my side, life would've been far harder and a lot less joyful."

"We must not allow ourselves to be overcome with emotion," Polly said in a strained voice. "Or we shall not hear the end of it from your Mama."

Lilly giggled. "She is resting inside."

Polly grinned. "I believe that moving into a cottage with sunlight will do her a world of good. And my grandmother, too."

"Indeed. The two of them shall be quite content in each other's company."

"Or they will be bickering like hens all day." Polly gave a slight shake of her head, an amused smile tugging on the edge of her lips. "Your poor Papa will have to keep the peace."

"I am sure he is up to the task."

Chapter Seven

"I do enjoy spending time with Shelly," Lilly said with a smile. She looked up at her mother, who was sitting across from her at the kitchen table, eyes squeezed shut. "She is everything a young lady ought to be."

Not only was Shelly in possession of a keen and sharp mind, but she was also cultured and well-read. Having been given the chance to travel frequently as the daughter of a gentleman, she had been exposed to all sorts of people and cultures. Furthermore, because of her mother's social standing, many people had known who

Shelly was before she had been presented to society.

And her presentation had been a glorious event.

Shelly herself had insisted on inviting both Lilly and Polly, who'd spent days in a frenzy. In the end, the two of them decided to make their own dresses and had spent long hours labouring over them until they were no longer able to keep their eyes open. By the sixth day, the two of them were ready, and were escorted to the event by the Blooms themselves. Mrs. Bloom, in particular, had taken a keen interest in Lilly and her miraculous tale.

All of polite society was abuzz with the news of Lilly's newfound wealth. Several times a day, when she was out and about with her mother, people approached her and asked her about the truth of the matter. Many of them were disappointed with her answers, and it showed on their faces. Others insisted on accompanying her to the shops or to the park, much to Rosie's dismay. Every night during dinner, the Chalmers puzzled over the matter and did their best to find the missing puzzle piece.

Alas, it had been months since they had left their old life behind, and any inquires Lilly made had amounted to nothing. Why, she'd even taken it upon herself to hire an investigator, paying him a handsome sum to uncover the truth, but he'd returned empty handed. So, the mystery of her change in circumstance remained as elusive as ever.

And Lilly herself became something of an enigma in polite circles.

While they did welcome her, given her close ties to the Bloom family, she knew that they regarded her as something of an oddity. Every party she attended was full of whispers and gazes that lingered too long. She tried to enjoy the music, the glittering chandeliers, and the wide array of food being served, but she could not help but feel as if she did not belong.

Lilly had grown up in a modest household where the Chalmers tended to everything themselves. To go from working until the late hours of the night to put food on the table to being waited on at grand parties thrown by the city's wealthiest and most affluent was nothing short of unnerving. Somehow, Lilly always ended up feeling as if she was an imposter, like someone would be able to point her out, and she would be dragged out and tossed out onto the street.

And it was a ridiculous notion.

No one rejected her to her face.

Instead, it was all polite smiles and curious gazes, and Shelly, in particular, had taken Lilly under her wing. During the occasions when Polly herself could not attend, having filled up her days and nights with work and her education, Lilly found herself in the company of the Bloom family's pride and joy. Unlike her, Shelly was born to be a debutante, always looking the part without a wayward strand of hair in sight, and green eyes that sparkled with warmth and humour.

Everyone adored her, and many men fell all over themselves in order to impress her. Since their arrival some hours ago, the two of them had been surrounded by a steady stream of men, all clamouring for Shelly's attention. Ever gracious and kind, she bestowed her attention upon all of them equally, and insisted on introducing Lilly as her dear friend. In truth, the two of them had become fast friends, with Shelly helping Lilly navigate the labyrinth of her new role, and Lilly bringing some much-needed wisdom and humility to Shelly's life.

The two of them made an odd pair and were regarded with no small amount of amusement, but Lilly found she could not bring herself to care. Not when she danced until her feet hurt, and her cheeks were flush with colour. Not when Rosie's health began to return little by little, with Peter having taken up gardening as a hobby, and certainly not when Polly and her grandmother kept them all company and filled their cottage with laughter and love.

It was an unusual situation, but Lilly would not have it any other way.

With a shake of her head, Lilly reached for another refreshment and took a few sips of the fruity drink. She set it down on the table and peered at Shelly, who was twirling away on the dance floor, unaware that she was the centre of attention. Lilly smiled when she caught Shelly's gaze and waved. Her friend threw her head back and laughed, and the man who was dancing with her looked smitten.

Poor fool.

Shelly had become important to Lilly, and while she doted on her friend, she knew that her capricious and lofty manner was sure to cause problems in the future. For now, with it being her first season, she was given the benefit of the doubt, but it would not be long before Shelly was expected to behave in a certain way, and all of her oddities were looked on as cumbersome rather than charming.

Lilly prayed it would not be too hard for Shelly to adapt.

When Mr. Bloom stepped into her field of vision, Lilly gave a start and nearly spilled her drink. "Mr. Bloom, forgive me. I did not see you."

Simon Bloom stood before her, in his dark tailored suit and vest and a tailcoat. He tilted his head in her direction and offered her a bright smile. "How do you do, Ms. Chalmer?"

Lilly jumped to her feet and curtsied. "I am well, thank you, Mr. Bloom."

"You look to be in good spirits," Mr. Bloom commented, his bright eyes wide and warm. "Are you enjoying the party?"

Lilly nodded and clasped her hands behind her back. "Very much, sir."

"She is too shy to dance," Mrs. Bloom interrupted from next to her. The old woman lifted her head up and looked directly at them, her eyes white and unseeing. "We must encourage her to dance."

Mr. Bloom nodded. "Indeed, you must."

Colour rose up Lilly's neck. "I am afraid I have not learned how."

Mr. Bloom took a seat next to his mother and twisted his head in her direction. After a moment, Lilly sat back down and folded her hands in her lap. Around her, the party continued, with people moving back and forth across the dance floor, surrounded by music and the rise and fall of conversation. Several doors were thrown open, allowing the smell of wildflowers and the crisp night air to waft in.

Lilly could think of nothing else on this fine night.

Except if her parents and Polly were in attendance.

But she knew they did not feel comfortable, so she had not pushed them. She imagined the four of them gathered around the fireplace, swapping stories and partaking in a fine meal. Abruptly, Lilly sat up straighter and ran a hand over her face, pushing away the melancholy.

"Forgive me, Ms. Chalmer, but you look troubled."

Lilly blinked and glanced over at Simon, firelight glistening on top of his head. "Not at all, Mr. Bloom. I am thankful to be here."

Mr. Bloom studied her face. "You are not used to such affairs."

Lilly smiled. "I am not, but I hope that in time, I will be."

"You look so much like your mother," Mr. Bloom murmured in a gentle voice. "It is quite unnerving. Forgive me, but I have been told that you are a relative of the Chalmers…"

Lilly stiffened, and her heart jumped into her throat. "They are the only parents I have ever known. I have been most fortunate and blessed to be raised by them."

Mr. Bloom cleared his throat. "Of course, I did not mean to imply otherwise."

Lilly studied his profile and ignored the pounding of her heart. "You knew my mother?"

Mr. Bloom sat up straighter and looked away from her. "I knew her a long time ago. She was a fine woman."

"Did you know my father, too?"

Mr. Bloom's mouth pressed into a thin white line. "I did."

"Will you tell me about them?"

Mr. Bloom looked back at her, and his expression grew pained. "Perhaps I will someday, but my memory is not what it used to be, and I do not wish to disappoint you."

Lilly swallowed. "I do not believe you are capable of disappointing me."

Mr. Bloom frowned at her. "You are too kind, Ms. Chalmer, but I am."

Lilly offered him a small smile. "In any case, I should be glad of anything you can tell me. My parents do not speak of the matter, because they find it to be too painful."

"It can be," Mr. Bloom murmured, a shadow moving across his face. "I am certain that you were well loved and cherished."

Lilly's throat turned dry. "Thank you."

"Your mother, in particular, was a kind soul and in possession of the sweetest temperament," Mr. Bloom continued, a sad smile hovering on the edge of his lips. "I was sorry to hear of her passing."

A lump rose in the back of Lilly's throat. "Thank you."

"If you are ever in need of anything, Ms. Chalmer," Mr. Bloom began, his eyes moving over her face with a strange intensity. "I am at your service."

"I am truly humbled and honoured, Mr. Bloom. I am quite content, and I am not in need of anything save for your daughter's friendship."

Mr. Bloom smiled. "I am glad to hear it."

Being Shelly's friend meant spending some time in the gentleman's company, but she could not understand his interest in her. Now and again, she felt his eyes on her, studying her, and although she often longed to ask him, she thought it better if she did not. Given that he was exceedingly fond of his daughter and lavished her with love and attention, it was likely that Mr. Bloom took an interest in her, because he wished to assure himself of her character. With the two of them spending time together, it was only natural that he wondered as to the true nature of his daughter's friend.

She had nothing but respect and admiration for the gentleman, and she knew he wished her no harm. On the contrary, Mr. Bloom had been nothing but welcoming and kind since her entrance into society, and his wife and mother even more so. The Blooms, as a whole, had taken a strong liking to her, and she found herself grateful for the guidance and the affection.

How fortunate she felt to have been blessed in such a manner!

"We must make her formal introduction to society," Mrs. Bloom announced in a louder voice. "Ms. Chalmer is deserving of such a thing, is she not? After all, you knew her parents, and she comes from a good family."

Mr. Bloom nodded, a thoughtful expression on his face. "Indeed. You are quite right, mother."

Mrs. Bloom reached across the table for Lilly's hand and patted it. "You ought to be a debutante, my dear. You and Shelly will take the London season by storm, I am sure."

Lilly blushed. "I cannot ask such a thing of you, Mrs. Bloom. You have given me too much already…"

Mrs. Bloom waved her comment away. "Nonsense. I will take care of the matter personally."

Weeks later, Lilly stood at the top of the stairs in a golden gown made of silk. At the bottom of the stairs, the Blooms awaited her, all of them wearing equally nervous and excited expressions. In the background, several people lingered, while everyone else milled about the estate, eager for her formal presentation into society.

Why did Lilly feel as if she was about to submit to a fit of the vapours?

She sucked in a deep breath, released it, and held her head high. Then she saw Polly wedge herself in between Shelly and Mrs. Bloom. In her silver gown with her hair piled atop her head, she was a vision, and it was all the confidence Lilly needed to climb down.

By the time she reached the bottom of the stairs, the music swelled and conversation rose around her. She came to a complete stop and lowered her head, allowing the attention to wash over her and trying not to pay any attention to the knots tightening in her stomach. As soon as she glanced back up, a few men had already gathered around her, all of them eager to make her acquaintance.

She caught Shelly's gaze, and the young woman grinned at her.

For the rest of the night, Lilly drifted from one partner to the next, twirling underneath the moonlight until her feet hurt. When she came to an abrupt halt, breathless and cheeks flushed with colour, Shelly whisked her away to a table near the food. Abruptly, she sat down and resisted the urge to groan.

Her days as a seamstress had not prepared her for such an event.

Why, she half preferred the silence, comfort, and familiarity of their sitting room, with the needle between her fingers and a fire crackling in the background. She listened closely, almost expecting to hear her mother calling for her, only to find that Polly had come to stand in front of her. She smiled at Lilly before taking a seat next to her and adjusting the folds of her dress around her.

Couples danced past, a blur of colour and movement.

Music continued to fill every inch of the room.

Lilly felt as if she were in a dream, and she could not decide if she wished to wake up in the familiar confines of the sitting room and the sound of her father's snoring a few feet away, or if she wished it all to continue. Surely, such a change was not meant to last forever, and Lilly could not help but feel as if she were holding her breath.

Awaiting it all to be snatched away.

Fiddlesticks. You have done nothing wrong. You deserve to be here, Lilly. Considering your change of circumstance, you ought to be enjoying your parties and everyone's praise.

While she did not know what to make of the gentlemen who had tried to catch her eye, she was nevertheless flattered and did not wish to offend them. So, she sat up straighter and smiled at those who gestured to her. Shelly came to sit opposite her and leaned in to whisper into Lilly's ear.

"I daresay this has been a success. You must be relieved."

"Relieved?"

Shelly leaned back and patted her hand. "I could see how nervous you are. You needn't worry. You looked radiant, and everyone talked about how well you carried yourself."

Lilly loosened a deep breath. "I am most relieved to hear it."

Shelly giggled. "As am I. I admit I was quite nervous on your behalf. I do not know why. You are such a natural."

Lilly twisted to face her and smiled. "Nonsense. I was sure I was going to fall flat on my face and embarrass myself."

"You have not."

"The night is young," Lilly pointed out with a shake of her head. "I would not celebrate just yet."

"There are many men here who would be more than happy to come to your rescue," Shelly pointed out, a mischievous twinkle in her eyes. "I do believe a few of them believe themselves to be in love with you already."

Lilly blushed. "Oh, do be serious."

Shelly turned her head and held her gaze. "I am being serious, Lil. Can you truly not see how they follow you around the room? Or their admiring gazes?"

Lilly raised an eyebrow. "You flatter me, and you give me far too much credit."

Shelly frowned. "And you do not give yourself enough credit. You deserve to be here, no matter what you think, and I, for one, am glad you are."

Sometime later, Polly was forced to take her leave of them. The two of them escorted her into the carriage, with Mr. Chalmer waiting inside. He gave his daughter a quick hug before they left, leaving her at the mercy of Shelly.

Unfortunately, now that she had come out into society, Shelly insisted on introducing her to all of polite society. Time passed slowly while she was dragged from one group to the next, with Shelly chattering and smiling the entire time. Lilly tried not to get swept up in the moment, and she kept her wits about her, particularly when she felt one particular young man staring at her from across the room.

"You seem to have caught the eye of Mr. Knightly," Shelly commented sometime later. The two of them were in the powder room, tending to their appearance. Eyes wide and full of life, Shelly turned to Lilly and pulled her in for a hug. "You cannot imagine how happy I am for you, Lilly."

Lilly hugged her back. "I am happy to be here. This is truly all so overwhelming."

Shelly drew back and fussed over Lilly's appearance. "You will get used to it, I am sure. I have never seen anyone handle it with as much grace and poise as you have."

"You are far too kind," Lilly murmured, a lump rising in the back of her throat. "Thank you for being my friend. Without your kindness and your acceptance, I do not know what would have become of me. Truly, you and your whole family have been so welcoming."

"I hope you know that we all consider you to be family," Shelly told her with a bright smile. "And I think of you as a sister."

And she could not have been more thankful to them.

For the life of her, she could not understand why they had taken pity on her, particularly when so many others had shunned her. Many members of society openly gawked, wondering what she had done to come into possession of such a fortune. After months, Lilly was still talked about, especially now that she was a member of polite society. As far as many were concerned, she was a long-lost relative, having been lost to time and misfortune before being restored to her rightful place.

Perhaps there was some truth to that sentiment.

Either way, Lilly found she did not care. Not when she had been given such a strange and beautiful opportunity. Adapting to this new life was going to take some time, but between her parents and Polly on one hand, and the Blooms on the other, she was sure that it was only a matter of time before she became another member of the city's well-to-do.

By next season, Lilly was sure they would scarcely remember all of the rumours being circulated. In the meantime, she needed to keep her head high and enjoy the present moment with all of the wonder and opportunity it held. Suddenly, Shelly took Lilly's hand in hers and steered her towards the door. Through the slit, they observed the people coming and going, dressed in subdued colours, and entirely fixated on each other.

How surreal the entire affair was.

"There." Shelly pointed, her voice scarcely more than a whisper. "Mr. Knightley is the gentleman standing by the refreshment table."

Lilly peered, and her heart gave an odd little twinge when the gentleman in question turned to the side, and his lips lifted into a smile. His hair was an unusual shade of auburn which caught the light when he moved. His hazel eyes were full of warmth and intelligence, and there was something pleasing and gentle about his entire manner. In his dark tailored suit, vest, and tailcoat, he was easily the most handsome man in the room, and a wave of butterflies erupted in her stomach at the thought of him.

Could Shelly be right?

Did Lilly dare hope a man of his calibre would take notice of her?

"He has been staring at you all night," Shelly continued in a higher voice. "I have noticed him, and I have been trying to tell you, but I did not wish to frighten you."

"Frighten me?"

Shelly twisted to face her. "You said yourself you are not used to being paid attention to, particularly not when it comes to men. I did not wish for you to become self-conscious and awkward in your manner and way of speaking."

Lilly breathed a sigh of relief. "It is good that you did not tell me, but what am I to do with this now?"

"Nothing," Shelly replied, offering her a kind smile. "You are not to do anything but smile and laugh at his jokes. In due time, Mr. Knightley will make his true intentions known."

"And what of the gentleman with him?"

"Mr. Price." Shelly's gaze drifted away, and she peered through the slit. "He is one of the most eligible bachelors in all of London. Heir to a grand estate, but he has been on society for years and has not once expressed interest in any of the young ladies."

"I do believe that is about to change."

Shelly's head whipped around, and she stared at Lilly. "What can you mean?"

"I have seen the way he looks at you. He is quite smitten, Shell. You have not noticed?"

Shelly's cheeks turned red. "Do not tease me so, Lil. Mr. Price would never take notice of me. Not when there are so many other eligible and cultured women here. I have not been out of leading strings for long…"

Lilly reached for Shelly's hand and squeezed. "You are one of the most accomplished young women in polite society. You are in possession of a keen mind and have the ability to set people at ease. You are also kind and good. What man would not want you as his wife?"

Shelly squeezed her hand back. "You are too kind, Lilly, but I am afraid I must not get my hopes up. Not unless I wish to spend the rest of the season pining after him."

"You will not," Lilly maintained.

With that, she took Shelly's hand and led her back outside. Quickly, the two of them sought shelter next to a set of doors overlooking the dance floor. Mrs. Bloom materialized out of thin air, her lady's maid in tow, and she lowered herself onto a chair, gripping her cane with both hands.

"I hope the two of you are enjoying yourselves," Mrs. Bloom announced. "I have heard talk of how successful the two of you have been so far."

Lilly and Shelly exchanged an excited look.

"It is expected that the two of you will find suitable matches and be married before the end of the season."

Lilly blinked. "Surely that is too short of a time to decide such a thing."

Mrs. Bloom sat up straighter, her gaze wide and unblinking. "When it came to Mr. Bloom, I knew right away. As soon as we set eyes on each other, it became clear to me that I could not marry anyone else."

Shelly sighed. "How romantic."

"Keep your wits about you," Mrs. Bloom warned, her eyes tightening around the edges. "Not every man you meet is a gentleman."

"Do not worry, grandma," Shelly assured her, before bending down to press a kiss to her cheeks. "Lilly and I will keep our wits about us."

"And we will not allow ourselves to be swept up in emotion," Lilly finished with a grin. The two girls burst into giggles, and Mrs. Bloom scowled in their direction. Shelly linked her arm through Lilly's and led her back onto the dance floor. Immediately, Mr. Knightley and Mr. Price found them and led them away to dance.

It had been the most magical night of her life.

***

Some five months later, Lilly was visiting Shelly when Mr. Knightley came to call on her. Shelly gave her a bright grin before moving to the other side of the drawing room and pretending to take an interest in the pianoforte. As soon as Mr. Knightley walked in, Lilly's knees went weak, and the butterflies in her stomach erupted into a frenzy.

Over the past few months, they had seen more and more of each other. While he had not made her an offer of marriage, his intentions towards her were clear. Why, even Mrs. Bloom spoke as if the matter was already done. Together with Shelly, the two of them spent many hours fawning over Lilly and discussing her wedding.

Yet, Mr. Knightley himself had not discussed the matter directly.

During the course of their courtship, whether they were on long walks in the park, with Shelly's lady's maid serving as a chaperone, or during the endless stream of parties they attended, Mr. Knightley did not discuss the topic. Instead, they spoke of anything and everything they could think of, including how Lilly came to be in possession of a fortune. Having satisfied himself with her answer, Mr. Knightley did not bring the topic up again, for which she was immensely thankful.

Time and again, he had proven himself to be nothing short of a gentleman.

He'd even taken an interest in her parents and the Wodehouses, taking it upon himself to call on her often and bring them all treats. Already, her parents adored him and impatiently awaited the day he asked her to become his wife. In truth, Lilly herself was beginning to grow worried, wondering if Colin Knightley had changed his mind about her. On several occasions, she had been tempted to ask, but she was encouraged not to by Shelly, who had assured it would only have the adverse effect.

A lady did not beg a man to make his intentions clear.

"You look beautiful as always, Ms. Chalmer," Mr. Knightly said, before tilting his head in her direction. He held out the flowers and smiled at her. "I could not come calling without a gift."

"You are always bringing me gifts," Lilly pointed out, before pausing to sniff the flowers.

She handed them over to the maid, who dipped her head and disappeared. "You are too kind, Mr. Knightley."

"You are looking well, too, Ms. Bloom," Mr. Knightly said over his shoulder. Shelly murmured a greeting, pretending to be engrossed in the music. She stood up, pushed the window open, and the smell of wildflowers poured into the sitting room. Outside, the sun was high in the sky, nary a cloud in sight.

Lilly's eyes swept over the room, from the cream-coloured walls to the couch overlooking the fireplace. Finally, she took a seat on the chair across from Mr. Knightley, who took off his hat and set it down on the couch next to him. Over the next hour, the two of them talked in hushed tones, while the rest of the world ceased to exist. When a tray of tea and biscuits were brought in, Mr. Knightley stood up and came to stand directly in front of her.

"What is the matter?"

Mr. Knightley got down on one knee and reached for her hand. "I have a very important question to ask you, Ms. Chalmer, and I do hope you will accept."

Over his shoulder, she saw Shelly press her lips together, and her entire expression lit up. Lilly inched closer to the edge of the seat and ignored the pounding of her heart. Slowly, she lowered her gaze to meet his, and her throat turned dry.

"I have never met a woman who is more my equal. For years, I have searched and searched, believing that I would never find her," Mr. Knightley began, his eyes filled with emotion. "Now that I have finally found you, I cannot wait one more moment to call you my wife. Would you do me the great honour of accepting my hand in marriage?"

Lilly's eyes filled with tears. "I would be honoured to become your wife."

That night, the Chalmers, the Blooms, and the Wodehouses came together in celebration of Lilly's joyous news. When she retired for the night, Lilly could scarcely sleep, because her heart was so full of joy. A week later, on a warm spring day, with Lilly and Colin trailing behind, Mr. Price got down on his knee in the middle of a park full of people and asked Shelly to become his wife.

Lilly's happiness could not have been more complete.

Together, the two of them planned for their weddings to be only a few weeks apart. The Blooms spared no expense for either of them. Every night, Lilly went to sleep with a fullness in her heart and a spring in her step. During the day, she spent time with Polly, who had secured a position as assistant to a shopkeeper, thanks to the generosity and kindness of the Blooms. Little by little, the Chalmers and the Wodehouses came to life again in the cottage, with Rosie's health in particular becoming better and better.

So much so that her mother insisted on making the wedding dress herself.

With the help of Polly, the two of them spent days and nights tending to the dress, refusing to allow Lilly to lift a finger to assist them. So, she took it upon herself to see to other details, including Shelly's own wedding dress. Thankfully, with their weddings weeks apart, the ladies were free to assist each other. Lilly was to be wed first and honeymoon in Paris, returning two weeks later in order to attend Shelly's wedding. Afterwards, Shelly was to vacation for a few weeks before returning home as a married woman.

In her wildest dreams, Lilly could not have imagined such a fate for either of them. Gone was the girl who had spent her days tending to dresses and dreaming of adventure and romance. In her stead was a young lady on the cusp of womanhood, about to embark on the great adventure of her life with the man of her dreams by her side. Mr. Knightley was everything she had hoped for and more, and she looked forward to spending the rest of her days by his side as his wife.

On the day of her wedding, it was Peter who insisted on walking her down the aisle in spite of his limp. As they walked side by side, Lilly could not help but feel as if the rest of her life had been building up to this moment and everything that awaited her henceforth.

Lily came to a stop in front of Colin and sent up a quick prayer.

An entire lifetime of happiness was hers for the taking.

And what a strange journey it had been to get there!

Sample from "The Redhead Baby" by Sophia Watts

Polly Cross had never wanted for anything in her life.

Being the only child of a wealthy merchant and his genteel wife of noble birth, she had always known a life of privilege afforded to her due to her family's social standing. She was especially grateful to have been given such opportunities, considering her sex. Indeed, many of the other families surrounding their country estate, nestled on the outskirts of the English countryside, had shaken their heads at her with disapproval written in their eyes. As a young girl, she had spent far too much time caring for their opinion and sought to improve upon herself.

Until she realized it was of no use.

After all, she was first and foremost a woman, and although her parents doted on her and often ignored societal expectations, she still knew what was expected of her. Being friends with many of the other young ladies of her station made her privy to such information, and she knew that it was only a matter of time before her parents came to their senses. In time, she too was to be presented like a prized horse to be examined and prodded by a selection of eligible suitors. In truth, Polly dreaded the coming of that day, two years hence, and she found herself growing quite melancholy at the thought.

Luckily, it was her companion, Sophie Ward, who came to her rescue during such hard and troublesome times. Why, if it were not for the dark-haired girl with kind hazel eyes, a quiet voice, and unwavering loyalty, Polly was not at all sure as to what she would have done. The daughter of their cook, Sophie, was very much the sort of girl who preferred her own company and that of her mother to anything else. On several occasions, she had tried to reason with Polly regarding the folly of her ways, particularly as she had grown older and wilder.

Bless her heart.

Polly was not unaware of her childhood friend's worry and the way her gaze lingered on her, but she found she did not have it in her to indulge her. At least not all of the time. Instead, she took as many opportunities as she could to run barefoot all over the estate, with her dark hair whipping in the wind and her jade green eyes full of mirth and mischief. During those moments, Sophie would trail after her, her hands clasped behind her back and eyes tight with disapproval.

Poor Sophie.

She did not know what it was to want, to crave something else with every fibre of her being. Polly, on the other hand, was all too familiar with such feelings. Having grown up in a lavish house with her every desire to tend to, she supposed she ought to be more grateful. And she was. But she could not help but feel that there was more to life than being left to her own devices. With her father mostly away on business and her mother busy with entertaining guests in her drawing-room, Polly was more often by herself. It was precisely why Sophie had been employed as her companion once she became of age. She suspected that her parents did not wish to burden themselves with such thoughts, or they would be forced to face their own guilt. Neither could she fault them for resorting to such measures.

On the contrary, she understood perfectly why it needed to be done. Polly was nothing if not astute, and having spent her entire life adhering to a routine, she understood the necessity of some measures—to some degree. Still, she wished for adventure, for a life beyond the borders of their sprawling estate, a gilded cage with well-dressed keepers. It was not until she was eleven that she came to learn, quite by accident, the true nature of the circumstances under which she was brought into the world. Being of frail health and having little strength, her mother had suffered through the loss of several children before her arrival.

Two of them, young boys with dark curls and green eyes like hers, had died upon contracting a strange illness when they were scarcely two years old.

Polly recalled discovering the portraits left in an empty room, hidden behind old furniture or covered by thick sheets. For hours, she had stayed in the cream-coloured room while she studied the portraits, tracing them over and over until Sophie had found her. The little girl had turned white as a sheet, tugged on her hand, and would say nothing until the two of them were outside near the stables. In a daze, Polly had listened to her friend recount the tale told to her by her mother in the hopes of avoiding such a thing from reoccurring. Afterwards, Polly had walked back into the house and straight up to her room.

There, she resided for three days, refusing all manner of food and refreshment. Sophie remained by her side, refusing to leave except for short stretches of time to eat and assist her mother in the kitchens. By the third day, it was her parents who came to find her, having received the distressing news from the housekeeper, Mrs Goodwin. A woman of five and forty, Mrs Goodwin had been employed by her family for quite some time and was adept at her job. The Cross household was in extremely capable hands. The woman's dark hair, which was peppered with streaks of grey, tight brown eyes, and a mouth that rarely smiled, resulted in Polly often avoiding the older woman at all costs.

Upon taking to her bed, however, she had no choice but to deal with her. Mrs Goodwin was firm but far kinder than Polly had anticipated. And it was with a sigh that she dispatched a letter to the Master and Mistress of the house, urging them to return from their trip. So it was that Polly found herself being drawn into her mother's warm embrace, inhaling the scent of soap and jasmine. Her father, on the other hand, a tall and reserved man with hair the colour of sunshine, blue eyes like the ocean, and a reserved nature, patted her on the back and said nothing.

Although it was six years ago, Polly thought of that day regularly. She often turned it over and over in her mind, recalling the tears in her mother's green eyes as she recounted the truth, while her father placed a hand on her shoulder, his chin raised high. For the life of her, she had not been able to understand how they had overcome such tragedy with such grace and poise. Why, it confused her still, but she prayed that her siblings were in a better place and that her parents suffering may come to an end at long last. For a time, her wild and inquisitive nature had been tempered, as Polly had spent the next several years in the library with her head buried in books. She lost herself in stories of far-off lands whose names she could not pronounce, mythical creatures, and women who were masters of their own fate.

And what marvellous fun it was.

Polly was content until some months ago when she stumbled upon a young man with hair dark as a cloudless sky, kind brown eyes, and a bright smile. He had been standing outside, near the fountain, underneath the later afternoon sun when she happened upon him. Polly's head was filled with the sound of gurgling water, birds chirping in the background, and the distinct sound of her own heart pounding in her ears. Breathless, she approached the gentleman, dressed in a white muslin shirt tucked into dark trousers, and a blue tailcoat with golden buttons, and a top hat. Upon noticing her, he had straightened his back, tucked his hat underneath his arm, and offered her a low bow.

Michael Woodhouse was to be her father's new business partner.

Having inherited the mantle from his own father, she later learned that he had spent the past several years traveling from place to place, hoping to learn as much as he could about the business. Some months later, after his twenty-fourth birthday, he had returned to England with a head full of ideas and enthusiasm for the new venture. During dinner that night, her father spoke highly of him, going on at length about what a fine and admirable man he was, one who sought to be worthy of the fortune he had inherited and the responsibility that came along with it. By the dim light of the candle, she had watched her father speak of him in such glowing terms that she herself felt moved.

Only her feelings were of an entirely different nature.

Over the past few months, she had gone out of her way to make herself available at the house, all but giving up on her excursions altogether. And all just to catch a few brief glimpses of a man who kept her up at night, with a giddy feeling in the pit of her belly. Nowadays, she had taken to writing about him, composing long poems, only to be teased mercilessly by Sophie. Today, her father had insisted that she accompany them for a tour of the estate, trailing behind at a respectable distance while they spoke.

And what a glorious afternoon it was.

Mister Woodhouse was certainly unlike any man of her acquaintance, and of all her father's associates, she liked him the best. He had proven himself to be a kind and thoughtful man, eager to leave his mark on the world and to leave it a far better place than how he found it. Polly was more and more in danger of losing her heart to him entirely with each passing day. So consumed by the depth of her feelings for him, she did not notice that he, too, felt the same. It was with no small amount of shock that she received a letter from him, requesting the pleasure of her company sometime later that evening. With Sophie as her chaperon and with her parents' knowledge and blessing, Michael began to court her.

Now, a year later, at eighteen and twenty-five years of age, they were finally engaged.

Polly did not recall ever feeling such emotions. It was only a few hours prior that Michael had gotten down on his knees, taken her hands in his, and with the sprawling estate looming in the background, he had asked her to become his wife. With tears in her eyes and a heart full of love, she accepted, never wishing to be parted from him any further. Being forced to endure his absence for months had taken its toll on her, but with her beloved Michael back, and the two of them soon to be wed, she could not imagine a happier ending.

A month later, with their family and friends in attendance, the two of them were wed in the country church, with Michael cutting a handsome figure in his suit while Polly wore a white dress made of the finest muslin and a smile that lit up her entire face. Afterwards, they led their guests to the Cross country estate, and there the true festivities began. People laughed, drank, and danced well into the night. Meanwhile, the new couple sat in a quiet corner giggling and exchanging loving glances, with their hands interlaced and a bright moon over their heads.

Three weeks later, she happened upon Michael bent over his desk, with one hand through his hair and the other holding a drink. Tentatively, she approached him, heart hammering against her chest. When she laid a hand on his shoulder, he did not react, save for a sharp intake of breath.

"What is it?"

"I am to leave in two days," Michael replied in a thick voice.

Polly swallowed. "When will you return?"

"I cannot say." Michael covered her hand with his. "But I shall make haste and return as soon as I can, my love."

Trouble had been brewing for some time. She had heard her father and husband discussing the matter in hushed tones behind the locked doors of her father's study, surrounded by a thick plume of smoke and the smell of aged pine. With what little tidbits she had gathered, she was able to determine that there was to be a war between the Anglo-Chinese and British soldiers due to the opium trade in the east. Polly had lived in fear of the consequences of such a war, having spent the past few days tossing and turning. It did not come as a surprise to her when Michael finally spoke of it to her, but she had prayed for more time.

Yet, on the morning of his departure, Polly found herself rising before the first rays of light to ensure his breakfast was ready. Once prepared, she found herself drifting off into the drawing-room until she came to a stop in front of the window. A few miles down the road, the top of her parents' estate was visible, and she pictured them embracing each other warmly by the light of the fire, only exchanging a few loving words. With a shake of her head, she pushed the thought away and listened to the familiar creak in the floors beneath her. She hurried out of the drawing-room and into the hallway, meeting Michael by the foot of the stairs. He pressed a kiss to her forehead and brushed past her and into the dining room. There, she took a seat next to him and adjusted the folds of her light blue dress around her.

When breakfast was done, Michael lingered, holding onto her hands with both of his. "I do not wish for you to worry, my darling. Your every need will be tended to."

"I wish you did not have to go."

Michael exhaled. "Nor do I. It has been barely three weeks since we have been wed, but I fear I must go. It is my duty."

Polly's throat turned dry. "Will you write to me?"

"As often as I can, my darling."

"I will write to you every day," Polly promised, ignoring the knots tightening in her stomach. "And I shall eagerly await your return."

Michael gathered her into his arms. Then he pressed his lips to hers for a sweet kiss. A few moments later, he reluctantly drew back and pulled Polly up to her feet. He offered her one last hug before he took his leave. Polly stood rooted to the spot, but when she heard the clattering of hooves slowly subsiding, she raced to the front door and pulled it open. Before she reached the last step, she collapsed into a heap, the tears coming unbidden. When Sophie's familiar arms closed around her, she clung to her lady's maid, feeling suddenly spent and drained. With a great deal of difficulty, Sophie managed to coax her mistress back into the house and into her bed. The lady's maid left the curtains open, revealing a warm and bright day, before she tucked Polly's covers around her.

But Polly's condition only worsened...

Read more by visiting Sophia Watt's author page on Amazon today...

Printed in Great Britain
by Amazon

79717074R00109